LIFE,
INTERRUPTED

Praise for *Life, Interrupted*

'*Life, Interrupted* is a lovely, warm, funny book –
though searingly sad at times. I wish I'd written it.'

Jacqueline Wilson

'I loved this book – I thought it was loving and
evocative. The sad bits are heartbreaking and the
characters are real people we all know. This is an
important book that everyone should read.'

Eoin Colfer

'Sure-footed and perceptive, warm and funny and oh
so sad. The characters are absolutely living, breathing
beings. Damian writes completely from the heart, and
it shows.'

Vivian French

'Great fun to read. Damian has very cleverly written
a book about a very sad subject that somehow manages
to leave you feeling very happy.'

Charlie Higson

DAMIAN KELLEHER

LIFE, INTERRUPTED

PICCADILLY PRESS • LONDON

For Freddie

With thanks to Anne Clark, and my early readers,
Beth Miller and Sophia Khan.
And of course, to Kally and Sophie

First published in Great Britain in 2009
by Piccadilly Press Ltd,
5 Castle Road, London NW1 8PR
www.piccadillypress.co.uk

A catalogue record of this book is
available from the British Library

ISBN: 978 1 84812 003 7

1 3 5 7 9 10 8 6 4 2

Printed in the UK by CPI Bookmarque, Croydon, CR0 4TD
Cover design by Simon Davis
Cover illustrations by Sarah Kelly

Mixed Sources
Product group from well-managed
forests and other controlled sources
www.fsc.org Cert no. TT-COC-002227
© 1996 Forest Stewardship Council
FSC

chapter one

It all starts in the spring, which is odd when you think that spring is meant to be about growth and renewal. Mum likes spring because she loves daffodils, and she says when the little yellow trumpets start poking their heads above ground it always reminds her that sunshine is on its way. Mum's been complaining that she hasn't felt well for a couple of days. It isn't like her, but everyone at school's had this cold that's been going round. Even when she has a bad cold though, or the flu, Mum still carries on, getting up for work, pulling her pink dressing gown on and yawning as she heads for the bathroom, knowing the toilet seat will be up because she says that's what you get with two boys in the house.

This morning, she's getting ready to leave – got her nurse's uniform on already – but she's complaining of a pain in her shoulder. I start to give it a bit of a rub but, as soon as I touch it, she winces with pain.

'Ooh, careful, Luke, love,' she says. 'It's really tender there.'

'Call in sick,' I tell her. 'Say you're not well. You're not well.'

She gulps down a couple of paracetamol with a swig of tea.

'They're short-staffed as it is,' she says, fastening her watch. 'Half the hospital's got that nasty cold. Hope I'm not.'

'You want to go and see the doctor,' I tell her. 'The place should be crawling with them.'

'Doctors . . .' she scowls. Worked as a nurse for years, my mum. But she still doesn't trust doctors. Just the word is enough to set her teeth on edge.

'It's probably a bit of arthritis,' she says, as though a bit of arthritis is worth celebrating. We're sitting in the kitchen, drinking tea. I'll be off to school soon and she'll be off to work. Gospel Park hospital is a huge place, and Mum is a sister on the old people's wing, the 'geris', as she calls them, short for geriatrics. I've seen her at work with her patients. She teases them, has a joke with them, flirts a little with the old boys, has a laugh with the old girls. Their eyes burn brighter when she's around, and little lines crinkle up their faces as they smile. She makes time for them, she's good at her job.

'Don't go in today, Mum,' I say, buttering a slice of toast. 'I'll call if you like.'

'You've got school,' she says. 'I'm fine. I can't let the girls down.'

She always calls the rest of the nurses 'girls' though they're nearly all wives and mothers, and there are a couple of blokes, too. She rubs her shoulder with her right hand, but I can see her screwing up her eyes against the pain.

'Have you done your homework?'

Typical Mum. Diversionary tactic. Still, I can see she isn't going to stay off work today. I might just as well give up now.

'Yes,' I say. 'Well, most of it . . .'

'Right,' she says, holding up Jesse's lunchbox. 'There's his sandwiches. Make sure he doesn't leave them behind, will you? You know what he's like.'

Jesse's my younger brother, and yes I do know what he's like. He's a prat most of the time. Football mad. He gets to school half an hour before everyone else so that he and a few of his Neanderthal mates can kick a ball round a yard. I wouldn't mind but he's not that good. He won't eat school dinners (unlike me) because it's a waste of his valuable footie time. It's all he ever thinks of. It's all he talks about. Who's where in the league. Who's playing who. Who's been signed up by this or that club. Who's past their sell-by date. Football. Who cares?

Jesse often rushes out the door and leaves his packed lunch behind. So, of course, it's usually up to yours truly to take it in for him. To be honest, I'd leave it where it is on the table to teach him a lesson. Serve him right. But Mum always asks me to take it in for him, and I can't say no to her. She knows he won't come back for his lunch if he leaves it behind. Once he's started playing, that's the only thing on his mind.

That's Jesse for you. He'd rather keel over from malnutrition than stop playing football for five minutes. You can see it when he plays. Pure concentration on his face, eyes focused on the game. There's nothing else in the world that matters – nothing, and no one.

Not like me. Sport, I can take it or leave it, and I usually leave it unless it's the tennis or the wrestling. I don't mind football when it's a big match – the FA Cup final, the World Cup, that sort of thing – but I can't sit ogling Wycombe Wanderers against Berwick-upon-Tweed for a full ninety minutes as though my life depended upon it. Not like Jesse can. Me, I'd rather sit and listen to my music. Sometimes I do drawing, you know, sketching and that, though I can't say I've much talent. I've even been known to write the odd poem. I started when my dad left. It was horrible stuff really, but Mum encouraged me. She said it would help me cope with my feelings. We didn't hear from Dad for a few weeks. No cards, no letters, no calls, no nothing.

Well, that's not entirely true. The phone did ring a couple of times, and it was obvious there was someone there at the other end of the line, listening, not daring to speak, or maybe not able to. But I could hear him breathing. Not cranky or pervy. Just desperately trying to find the right words to say and desperately failing. That's when he'd hang up.

He's in Scotland now. We get a call at Christmas, a card for our birthdays, though it's usually a week late and he always writes 'sorry it's late' in his spidery scrawl on the back of the envelope. Sometimes there's even a call if he's been watching some family pap on the telly that's triggered an attack of the guilts.

'See you, love.' Mum pulls me towards her and pecks my forehead with a kiss. But I put my hand up against her shoulder, only lightly, and now she's screwing up her eyes again.

'Mum, you can't go in to work like this.'

'I told you, Luke, I'm fine.'

There's an edge to her voice, now. It's her no-nonsense, don't-tell-me-what-to-do voice.

'I may be late tonight, love,' she shouts. 'So many people off sick at the moment with this flu bug, I may have to cover if they need me. There's stuff in the freezer for you and Jesse. Don't forget to lock up.'

She's suddenly out of the door, and I can hear the car starting up. Jesse stomps into the kitchen. He's late.

'Where's Mum?'

'Like you care.'

He gives me one of his filthy looks.

'Gone to work. Just now.'

He kicks a chair.

'She hasn't washed my kit. Why hasn't she washed my kit?'

He holds up his football stuff from Sunday's game. It's covered in caked-in, dried-on mud. The stuff that washing-powder advertisers dream of.

'Tough. Maybe she forgot. She's not feeling great.'

He rams it in his Adidas bag, grabs an apple and rushes out the door, slamming it behind him.

I hold up his sandwiches.

'Don't forget your lunch . . .'

chapter two

If there's one thing I really hate, it's being pulled out of class. It's so embarrassing, humiliating. Everyone always thinks someone's died, or your house has been burned down, or you've been out mugging little old ladies. And that you've been caught.

Anyway, it's Cheryl Monroe from 11M who comes to yank me out. I hate Cheryl Monroe. She has that sneery look on her pug-dog face like she's picking up on a really bad smell, and she knows it just came out of your arse.

'Luke Napier. Mrs Halloran's office. Now.'

The heads swivel as though this is some weird spectator sport, and I'm the one about to be fed to the lions. I can feel my cheeks blazing like beacons. Oh God, she means me.

It's history so we've got Mr Mayer. You can see him sitting there sniffing the nicotine off his fingers from lunchtime and dreaming of his next fag.

'All right, Mr Napier. Off you go.'

Everyone's staring at me, fixing me with their 'what-have-you-been-up-to' eyes.

I get up from my desk and Cheryl Monroe is waiting by the door. She's trying to look nonchalant, pretending she's chewing gum. She isn't. We're not allowed to chew gum in class, and although Cheryl isn't actually in class at the moment, she's not silly enough to be caught out by a technicality like that.

'Put your books away, lad.'

Mayer has slipped a sympathetic, velvet-lined glove over his normally harsh tones, anticipating the mini earthquake that has demolished my home, or the sudden car crash that has deprived me of my nearest and dearest. Everyone is starting to look worried now. They're thinking something bad must have happened for Mayer to be so nice all of a sudden. I shove my books into my bag and move towards Cheryl Monroe. She's picking an imaginary fibre from her school cardigan now and flicking it on the floor. It's no more real than the gum she is chewing.

I close the door behind me.

'Come on, tortoise,' says Cheryl in a really sarky voice. 'Hurry it up. I'm missing art, thanks to you. Only half-decent lesson in this dump.'

Cheryl obviously feels that, at the age of fourteen, I

cannot deliver myself to our head teacher's office without her assistance. It's all part of her plan to take over the world, starting with Joan of Arc Comprehensive. I'm not impressed. Her black trainers squeak on the polished floorboards as she bounces along, happy in the knowledge that some sort of poo is about to hit the fan. She pulls up suddenly outside Mrs Halloran's office and raps sharply on the door in a strange, mannered way, like a bored member of cabin crew demonstrating the emergency procedure. Only Cheryl's display is all for my benefit. There's a muffled 'Come!' from within, and after struggling with the knob briefly, she makes her entrance and announces, 'Luke Napier' rather unnecessarily.

'Thank you, Cheryl, you may go.' Mrs H doesn't even look up. Cheryl puts her lips against my ear.

'It's that divvy brother of yours, knocked himself out. Waste of bloody space.'

Mrs Halloran finishes whatever she's writing (notes for the governors? Memos for the staff? Shopping list?), caps her fountain pen and looks up. She knows the game: I'm in charge. You'll wait. I'm the queen, you're the pawn. And it's my move. There's also an over-powering smell of perfume. I don't know what it is she uses, but it smells sickly and floral, a bit like fabric conditioner.

'Ah, Luke,' she says finally. 'Seems your brother has had a little mishap on the games field.'

I count to three.

'Again.'

I knew that was coming. Jesse's so accident-prone, he's a card-carrying member of casualty these days. There was the broken nose at Christmas (it wasn't, it just bled like it was), the sprained ankle when he slipped during ten minutes of freak snow in February, and then he cut his knee open about a month ago. Those were all football injuries. Plus there are numerous other little mishaps along the way. Still, they've never yanked me out of class before.

'What's he done this time, Miss?'

'Seems he may have knocked himself out.'

Mrs Halloran removes her glasses and perches them on top of her concrete hair do. They won't come down without a struggle.

'Playing football,' she adds, as though I might be thinking he was shot-putting or tossing the caber.

'We've tried getting hold of your mother, but to no avail.'

Mrs Halloran speaks in that strange way that only head teachers and newsreaders adopt, as though their grammar is constantly being monitored.

'She might be working a double shift,' I explain. 'They're short-staffed at the moment. Her mobile will be switched off.'

'You'd better go with him. To hospital. I'm sorry

but I can't spare a member of my staff on one disaster-stricken twelve-year-old.' She extracts the glasses from her hair, pops them back on her nose, and returns to whatever it is she's writing.

'He's eleven,' I say. 'He's not twelve until August.'

'The ambulance is waiting by the gates.' She doesn't look up. 'Chop chop.'

An ambulance. At school. How unbelievably uncool is that? I can now feel dozens of pairs of eyes burning into the back of my head as I climb up the steps to get in the ambulance. The bell's just gone for afternoon break, and a small crowd has gathered, though God knows what for. Inside, there's a paramedic sitting with Jesse. She's holding his hand and, oh no, how deeply humiliating, it looks as if he's been crying.

'Ah, is this Luke?'

I'm tempted to say 'No', and run for it, but I'm thinking of Mrs Halloran's beady eyes glued to the back of the ambulance and imagining her unleashing her bloodhounds to track me down.

'Yes. I'm his brother.'

Jesse has that 'Oh God, this hurts so much' look on his face, and his footie shirt is wet through with snotty tears.

'I'm Sam,' says the paramedic. 'We're just going to get Jesse to Gospel Park for an X-ray to make sure he's all right. Okay?'

I nod and smile in what I hope is an intelligent way.

'He's been knocked out for a minute or two, so we don't want to take any chances now, do we?'

I turn to Jesse.

'How d'you do it this time?'

Jesse grimaces, then takes a deep breath.

'Well, Ryan passed to Dan, and Dan started running up the wing . . .'

'The short version, Jesse.'

'I scored. Then I ran into the goalpost.'

I can't believe this. He's got a great smirk plastered right across his gob now.

'You prat.'

'Where's Mum?' He suddenly looks at me in desperation, like a heat-seeking missile in search of sympathy.

'Don't know. They tried to get her on the mobile. Maybe she's having a late lunch.'

It's unusual for Mum. Normally when she gets back from work she complains that she hasn't had time for lunch. 'Just snatched a cup of tea and some toast,' she says, standing in front of the fridge, scanning it for something to eat.

'I forgot my lunch,' moans Jesse, and I feel a small pang of guilt as I think of the sandwiches that I left on the side, thinking, that'll teach him a lesson.

Jesse looks like he's getting ready to snivel again. The

driver starts to put a bit of a spurt on, as if he can tell.

'Are you all right?' Sam asks, holding Jesse's hand as a tear manages to escape and starts rolling down his cheek. 'You'll be fine, big boy like you. Bet you've scored a few goals, haven't you?'

She's distracting the patient, excellent tactic. This girl's a pro. While Jesse starts explaining, yeah, he's scored a few but he's usually in defence, I have a good look around. It's like something out of some hospital drama: oxygen canisters, first-aid boxes, red blankets. The real McCoy.

'Have you ever had any dead people in here?' Jesse's big brown eyes have dried up and are wide open now. The paramedic looks slightly flustered.

'Jesse,' I say in a hoarse kind of whisper. I'm tempted to give him a sharp dig in the ribs, but I'm scared he might start up again with the waterworks.

'I was only asking . . .'

'Nearly there,' says Sam. 'Not far now.'

I suddenly realise it's quite small and cramped and warm in here, and we're going pretty fast and I don't like the speeding motion much. For some reason known only to my digestive system (and possibly my brain), I start remembering that nasty greasy lasagne and chips I bolted down at lunchtime. Not only can I remember it, I can almost taste it. And that's when I know I'm going to throw up.

By the time they're wheeling Jesse in, I'm looking worse than he is.

Sam says, 'Don't you worry. I've got a clean uniform here at the hospital.' She's sponging sick off her jacket. I'd been aiming at Jesse, but I missed by a mile.

As we head through the scratched, grey double doors that swish like big rubber mats, I spot Mum's best friend, Mia. She's another nurse. As she sees me, she does a double take.

'Luke? Luke? What are you doing here?'

She looks puzzled, her hand goes to her head. I think, I could ask the same of you. She should be on the geriatric wing with Mum.

'It's Jesse,' I say, nodding my head towards his wheelchair. 'He knocked himself out playing football.'

Mia sighs. 'Not again. Is he all right?'

'He looks fine,' I say. The paramedics have propped Jesse up in a corner with a bag of cheese and onion, a can of Fanta and a copy of some crappety football magazine. He's got a big smirk on now, an I've-got-the-afternoon-off-school kind of look as he happily swigs his fizz and practically inhales the crisps.

'Can you tell Mum we're here?' I ask.

Mia looks embarrassed.

'She'll want to see Jesse,' I add, while I think, actually, does anyone really want to see Jesse? Surely not. 'She always looks in on him,' I say. Mia knows this. She must have been through Jesse's injury stories a hundred times with Mum.

'Your mum's not on the geri ward, Luke,' says Mia. She takes my hand in hers. I know there's something up now. Nobody over thirty ever holds the hand of a teenager unless something really awful has happened. Or they're a bit dodgy, and Mia's not.

'She's been brought over here,' says Mia. 'I just looked in on her.' I can see the worry on her face. She's stroking my hand now. Oh God, I knew it was bad news.

'She's not very well, Luke. You mum collapsed on the ward this morning.'

chapter three

Mum's propped up in a bed, hair pushed back off her face, and she's wearing a regulation hospital nightie. God, I think, things must be bad if they've got her into one of those. She's always bringing patients' nighties home and washing them because she says the hospital ones are 'a disgrace'. From where I'm standing, I think she's right on that score.

Mum has her eyes closed. I walk up close to her and notice for the first time the little criss-cross network of lines over the corners of her eyes. She's asleep. I can tell by her light, regular breathing, but I want to reach out and touch her. She looks so weird sitting in that bed. I can't remember how many times I've seen her tucking up the old people like a mother tucking in her baby, lifting them, getting them comfortable, taking their temperatures and fiddling with the clipboards at the end of their beds.

Normally, it's while Jesse and I have been waiting for her to finish a shift. She always says, 'I won't be a minute. I just want to get so-and-so settled.' Then twenty minutes later, she finally manages to tear herself away. It doesn't seem right now, seeing her here in this bed.

I pick up her hand. Her hands are usually quite cold, but this feels warm, with soft skin and bony fingers. I wrap my fingers around hers, and give them a slight squeeze, very gently. I didn't really want to wake her, I just wanted her to know I was there. Well, okay, I suppose I did want to wake her.

Her eyelids flicker into life and she opens her eyes, fixing me with a smile.

'Luke . . .'

The word hangs between us and hovers there. She lifts her hand and strokes my face. She looks sheepish, embarrassed.

'What happened, Mum?'

'I don't know, love . . .' Her voice trails off. 'All I remember is this terrible pain in my shoulder. It was like a red-hot poker being plunged in. I think I must have passed out. Next thing I know, I'm flat on my back in here. Who told you I was here anyway?'

I explain about Jesse and tell her how I intercepted Mia. Mum grimaces while I speak. Jesse's casualty habit has never gone down that well with Mum. 'I put in enough hours in this place,' she always says, 'without

17

having to come back because of you.'

'What's the matter, Mum? What's wrong with you?'

She shrugs her shoulders, and then I see her wince with pain again.

'Don't know.' She sighs. 'Nobody knows yet. They're talking about doing some tests.'

'Tests?' I've heard Mum spit the word out often enough to know that it normally means bad news. 'Tests? What for?'

Mum closes her eyes momentarily. I'd say the pain was hitting her where it hurts. There's a little smear of sweat on her forehead now, a bit like condensation.

'Go and check on Jesse for me, would you?' she says.

'Jesse? He's all right. It's you I'm worried about. What about you?'

'I'll be fine,' Mum says. 'He's only little, Luke. Look after him. He's your brother.'

'He's a bloody liability, that's what he is,' I say. 'He's in and out of casualty so often now that they're making jokes about booking him his own bed. And he's not little – he's eleven and a half.'

'But he's very young for his age.' Mum starts to try and hoist herself up.

'What are you doing?'

'I can't sit round here listening to you moaning,' she says. 'I've got to see Jesse.'

Mum starts ferreting around as if she's about to move.

Suddenly there's a nurse standing at the end of the bed.

'And what do you think you're up to?'

She's a tall, elegant black woman with her hair in hundreds of tiny braids, and she stands with her arms folded. Oh-oh, looks like there's going to be a stand-off at the Gospel Park corral.

'It's my other son, Jesse,' says Mum, wiping her forehead. 'He's been admitted to casualty. Had an accident playing football. I've got to go and see him.'

The nurse raises one eyebrow. Nothing else on her face changes, just the eyebrow. How cool is that, I think, and make a mental note to practise it at home in front of the mirror. I imagine using that one at school on Mr Mayer. 'Napier, your homework seems to have gone AWOL.' Reaction? Raised eyebrow. Genius.

'Now listen to me, Patricia,' says the nurse (nobody calls Mum Patricia – it's always Patty or Pat). 'You're not a well woman. You of all people . . .' She breaks off here and unleashes a volley of tuts in Mum's direction. 'You of all people should know that you're here to get better. And that, my dear, means doing what you're told.'

'I'm a sister too, you know, over on geris . . .' Mum's objection doesn't cut any ice.

'That's exactly what I mean,' says Sister Calder. She's close enough for me to read her name badge now.

'You stay right where you are. Ten steps out of this

ward, you're flat on your back, and whose job's on the line? Well it ain't yours!'

Her eyes are blazing. I can see she's not to be messed with and Mum's picking up on the vibe too. Mum also knows she's right.

'That's all very well for you,' says Mum, not giving up without a fight. 'It's not your son in casualty.'

'No, you're right, it's not,' says Sister Calder. Her tone's softening a little. 'But I'll tell you what I'll do, shall I? I'm going into the office right now, I'm going to pick up the phone, and I'll call casualty to find out how . . .'

She leaves a gap for Mum to insert the name.

'Jesse.'

' . . . Jesse is doing. All right? But first you have to promise me to stay right here in this bed. No moving. No more getting any ideas about wandering round the wards in your nightie. Deal?'

She fixes Mum with a stern look. Mum knows she has no choice.

'Deal,' she sighs.

'Right, let's find out how Jesse is getting on, shall we?'

She turns away from Mum and throws in her parting shot.

'Funny kind of name for a boy . . .' she says, winking at me as she sets sail off up the ward.

I take Mum's hand and I squeeze it a bit. I can see she's upset.

'He'll be fine,' I say. 'He always is. I'll go and check on him if you like.'

'No, don't worry, love,' says Mum. 'Maybe later.'

She squeezes my hand back. Her hands feel colder now. Bad circulation.

'How was school today?'

'Okay, nothing much happening this morning. Then this afternoon I got dragged out of class and bundled into an ambulance to escort Jesse here.' I edit out the bit about throwing up over the paramedic. Nobody needs to know that.

'Don't let this interrupt your lessons,' Mum begins. 'Go and phone Jack now and find out if you've got any homework.'

Jack's a mate of mine. Well, my best mate, really. Mum loves him because he always comes top in everything, and he calls her Mrs Napier. My other best friend Freya calls her Patty, which isn't surprising as she calls her parents by their first names too. Mum's right though. If anyone is up to date with the homework, it'll be Jack. I check my watch: 5.48 p.m. He'll have done the lot by now, I reckon, and be logging on to play 'War and Retribution', the latest shoot-em-up that's doing the rounds.

Sister Calder is marching back up towards us now. She allows Mum a little smile.

'I've just spoken to casualty and your son's been

transferred to one of the children's wards,' she says. 'They're keeping him in overnight. Just as a precaution.'

'What's wrong with him?' asks Mum.

'Well, apparently he's eaten two fish pies and three bowls of jelly, so not much by the sound of things,' Sister Calder says, smoothing down the covers. You can tell she's good with the patients. 'Shall I get him to pop in and see you in the morning? The charge nurse on Churchill ward reckons he'll be able to come across after breakfast when he's seen the doc.'

Mum nods and Sister Calder strides off down the ward. 'Looks like old bossy drawers won't be letting me out of here tonight,' Mum says. 'At least Jesse's sorted for the night, anyway. Now, what are we going to do about you?'

'I'm fine,' I say. 'I've got my key. I can just go home.'

'You are not staying in that house on your own,' says Mum. 'You're not even fifteen. Anything could happen.'

I'm not happy about the way this conversation is going. I know what's coming next. I don't want to sleep on that rank mattress that Jack keeps under his bed. Not tonight.

'Stay at Jack's,' says Mum. 'Go on. Go and phone him now. Have you got your mobile on you?'

'Forgot it.'

She tuts. 'I asked Mia to bring mine over but she

must have got distracted. Get my purse out.'

Mum's looking at her locker. It's like something out of the 1950s. She's nodding her head in a way that indicates 'Get my bag out and take some change and make that call'.

That's how well I know my mum. I know what all her gestures mean. I know that when she purses her lips together tightly that means, 'Stop that now, I'm about to erupt.' Jesse and I call that one her 'volcano lips'. Highly dangerous. Tonight she has another look altogether. She closes her eyes and her eyelids flutter so gently, you almost wouldn't notice. I have an inkling this means that something, somewhere is hurting badly.

I'm down the corridor, holding my nose against the wave of antiseptic smells that are washing over me, heading for the phone. I'm confident about lying about the sleepover. I do need to sort out the homework though.

I insert the money and dial the number. It keeps falling through, making a tinny chink against the little metal scoop at the bottom.

There's an old geezer standing next to me in purple striped pyjamas, with the waist tied up with string. Only he hasn't tied it tight enough, and his todger is trying to escape, though he hasn't noticed yet. He's only a metre away, and I can smell the fags from where I'm standing.

'Lick it,' he says.

'What?'

He looks at me as if to say, you idiot. It's obviously an instruction.

'Lick the coin. Before you put it in.'

'Oh.'

I lick it. Disgusting, cold metallic taste, probably covered in superbugs.

This time I put it in and it stays. The old bloke smiles triumphantly.

A male nurse arrives and hooks him away by the arm.

'C'mon now, Bernie, you've had your ciggie. *Emmerdale* starts in a few minutes. Oh, look at you, you're all coming undone . . .'

'Always works,' he shouts over his shoulder as he's escorted away while his pyjama bottoms are yanked up.

Eventually Jack answers the phone. It always rings for ages in his house, as though they've got better things to do. In our house, as soon as it rings we all dive for it. Like we're bored out of our tiny minds.

'Jack?'

'What d'you want?'

That's what I like about Jack. Always straight to the point, never any small talk.

'It's me.'

I know he knows it's me. I'm the only person from school who ever calls him, apart from Mad Marty

Perrino and we don't want to go there.

'I'm in hospital.'

There's a pause. I can tell he's digesting this information. He's dead clever is Jack, but sometimes it's the simple stuff that catches him out.

'What's the matter? You ill or something?'

'No, not me.'

'Oh, it's that stupid knobhead brother of yours, isn't it? I heard he got pulped again on the pitch . . .'

'Yeah, listen, Jacks, have you done the geography homework yet?'

I already know the answer, but it seems rude not to ask the question.

'Yeah. Why?'

'What was it?'

'Dead easy. Glaciers and how they form. Then you have to do a diagram. Piece of piss.'

'Okay, what else?'

'English. We read some poem about daffodils and now we have to write twelve lines inspired by another flower. Only not carnations.'

'Why not? What's wrong with carnations?'

'Nothing. Only Mrs Blythe hates them, and apparently every year when she sets this homework she gets at least ten carnation poems. They remind her of evaporated milk. And funerals.'

Fine, I'm thinking, I'll do roses.

'What did you do?' I ask Jack.

'Roses.'

'Bastard! I was going to do those . . .'

'Tough, I've done mine. Anyway, you can copy the geography, but I'm not writing you another poem. Try hyacinths.'

'Why?

'They rhyme with plinths.'

'Look, I'll see you tomorrow, quarter to. That'll give me enough time to copy the geography, won't it?'

'Yeah, should do. But don't forget your poem. I'm not writing that, too.'

'So you said. Okay, laters.'

I could have told him about Mum, but I didn't want to somehow. Anyway, he'd have been part of the deception then, and this one's got to be all mine.

I head back to the ward. Mum has closed her eyes, but she's not sleeping.

'All set?' she says.

'All set. Back to Jack's tonight.'

'I must get something for Ruth when I get out.'

Hmm. I'll have to cross that bridge when I come to it. Ruth is Jack's mum. She and Mum are good friends. It all goes back to when Jack and I started nursery on the same day. They share a bottle of wine occasionally and start moaning about blokes, then laughing about blokes, and usually end up crying about blokes. It normally happens when Jack's dad, Colin, is out for the night with his mates. Jack and I make ourselves scarce and watch a DVD.

'You'll be home tomorrow, won't you?' I ask.

Mum opens an eye. It's looking like a real effort.

I can see Sister Calder heading towards us now with a little pill rattling around in a plastic cup. At least Mum will get some sleep tonight.

'Course I'll be home tomorrow,' says Mum. 'They won't be keeping me in here. I'll go mad. Anyway, I'll be right as rain by then.'

But I think we both know that isn't true.

chapter four

It's weird the noise the key makes as I turn it in the lock. I mean, it's not as though I haven't done it a thousand times before. But then, there was always going to be someone coming home at some time – Jesse and Mum. But tonight, here I am, letting myself in. No one home. No one coming home. Just me. I know if I really think about it I could freak myself out. Home alone, nightmare on Colbourne Way. I shut the door behind me with a nice heavy clunk. Then I slide the bolts across, top and bottom, and put the chain on for good luck. Ghosts, ghouls, vampires, burglars. That'll keep them out.

Now on any other day, I suppose this would be my idea of heaven. No Mum. No Jesse. Just me. I can stay up all night if I want. I can eat whatever I like – okay, we're all out of smoked salmon and caviar, but Mum's stocked up on the oven chips, and there is a particularly tasty-looking Americano pizza in the freezer with my name on it. So I whack the oven on (gas mark nine – you need a proper little inferno to get the old oven chips nice and crispy), kick off my trainers and I'm just flicking through the channels (news – depressing, *EastEnders* – deadly, some reality TV show set in an opticians, called *Sight for Sore Eyes* – dire) when something happens that I haven't anticipated.

The phone rings.

D'oh.

Now I have one of two options here, I reckon. I can answer it, or I can let it ring. Razor sharp, me.

My mind's desperately racing to try and weigh up these options while I've still got them. If I answer it, and it's for Mum, I'll have to think on my feet. If it is for me, end of problem. What if it's Mum checking up on me though? Or one of Jesse's prattish mates phoning to find out how he is?

I decide it isn't Mum. That sleeping pill will be kicking in about now, I reckon. She'll be keeping the rest of the ward awake with her snoring (it's that bad). No, she won't wake now till they shake her up at the crack of dawn tomorrow, with a cup of milky tea and a soggy slice of carpet-tile toast.

It's still ringing. On an impulse I pick it up. I decide to keep quiet and let the caller speak.

'Hello . . .'

'Hello.'

'Who's that?'

'Who's that?'

'Is this some kind of parrot convention line I've called by mistake?'

'Uncle Stu? Is that you?'

'Luke, of course it's me, you wally. Who'd you think it was?'

'I don't know. Could be anyone.'

Uncle Stu is Mum's brother, her baby brother as she always calls him. He's about ten years younger than Mum, and he's all right. She used to look after him when they were kids. She wiped his snotty nose, cleaned his dirty bum and stuffed his face with food. If he got bullied, she'd beat them up. She was older and tougher. A lot tougher.

'How you doing, kiddo?'

'Not bad, thanks, Uncle Stu. How are you?'

'Fine, fine. Well, you know, could be better. Work's not great . . .'

His voice trails off. In my experience, when an adult goes all quiet on you, this normally means only one thing. He's got something to spill, only he isn't going to tell. I'd have to drag it out of him. Adults are dead predictable like that. They want to share, but they like you to do all the hard work. I figure I'd better get trawling.

'What's up, Uncle Stu?'

'Nah, work is pants. I'm fed up. Need a change. Your mum around?'

I knew the conversation was going to take this particular direction sooner or later.

'She's, er . . .' I have to think sharpish. 'She's in the bath. Up to her neck in Radox. Had a bit of a day.'

Well, I can't tell him I'm home alone, can I? I mean, he may be all right, but if you let an adult in on a little secret like you've snuck off home for a little 'me' time, they're sure to rat on you. They just would.

'Yeah, well, she's not the only one,' Uncle Stu replies. 'Listen, I don't want to take up any more of your time, you probably want to get back to *CSI*. Tell your mum I just called for a chat. I'll give her a ring tomorrow.'

There's a gap. I'm feeling sorry for him. There's something in his voice telling me he really needs to talk.

'You can tell me if you like.'

'You what?'

'You know, if you've had a bad day. Get if off your chest. Sounds like your day was pretty stressful.'

I don't know why I'm saying this. I really want to get him off the line. But it's too late now. I've said it.

'Tell me about it.' Uncle Stu sighs. 'It's not every day you get made redundant.'

'Made redundant?' I didn't see that one coming. Uncle Stu's a translator, works for some language agency in Manchester. To be honest, we hardly ever see him, and, when we do, he never really mentions work.

'Seems there's not the demand any more. Cut backs and that. So they're laying three of us off. Well, at least I know it's nothing personal.'

'I'm sorry, Uncle Stu,' I say. 'Something else will turn up, though, won't it?'

'Course it will, kiddo.' I can hear him smiling. He's not one to mope, Uncle Stu. He'll get on with it. I'm feeling a twinge of guilt about lying to him about Mum, but at least I haven't added to his woes. He could probably do without that tonight.

'Go on,' he says. 'You'd best get on with your homework. Bet you haven't even started it yet, have you?'

'No . . .' my voice trails off. 'Yeah, I'd better get on with it.'

'Tell Patty I'll call her tomorrow. Might just go out and get pi—, er, drown my sorrows. No need to get up early for work now, is there?'

'See you, Uncle Stu.'

'Take care, Luke.'

I put down the phone and make sure it clicks. Blimey. He sounded cheerful – not. Still, I have enough troubles of my own.

My stomach rumbles loudly. It sounds like a whale about to give birth. God, I'm starving. Time to get the pizza on and crack open the oven chips. Tonight, I'm home alone. No Mum, no annoying little brother. Bloody brilliant. I stick my finger up my nose and pick away to my heart's content. Homework? Pah, I'll worry about that tomorrow. Right now I have a pressing engagement with a pepperoni pizza. And sod it, I'm going to put extra pineapple on top.

chapter five

The next morning is just the beginning of my troubles. For a start, I oversleep, which isn't surprising as I don't have Mum yelling up the stairs at me. Then again, I don't have to bang on the bathroom door either, telling Jesse to get a move on. But in the end, I'm so late that I just about manage to brush my teeth, wave a comb over my hair and wash my face, all at the same time, before grabbing my bag and heading off out.

I leg it up the road but I know I'll be logged – it's about quarter past nine by the time I get to school. There's this smarmy-looking prefect on the gate writing down the names of all latecomers. I can see him smile as I run up, bright red in the face and panting like a sumo on a treadmill. He licks his lips in anticipation. I can tell he loves this job.

'So that's 9.16 precisely for, um . . .'

He looks at me.

'Name? Class?'

'Napier. 10N.'

He passes me a chitty.

'We'll see you in detention, Napier. 4.15 p.m. sharp. And don't do it again tomorrow.'

I throw him my best insolent glare. He has the smug, self-satisfied look of a traffic warden about him. Not tonight, you won't, bum face, I think. Tonight I'm going to see my mum.

'Cutting it fine, aren't you?' Jack whispers as I sit down next to him.

I suddenly remember. English homework. A poem inspired by a flower. Or not, as the case may be.

'You have written your poem, haven't you?' Jack says. 'I mean, I did tell you last night, didn't I?'

'Yes, you told me, and no, I haven't done it. Not yet, anyway.'

Mrs Blythe strides into class, shuts the door behind her and approaches her desk.

'Congratulations – you've just run out of time,' Jack hisses.

I throw him my most desperate, piteous look.

'Oh, for God's sake, pass me your exercise book . . .'

I shove it towards him.

'Has anyone not done the homework?' asks Mrs Blythe, her lips reverberating as she speaks. Tuna Chops we call her, on account of the big fishy kissers slap bang in the centre of her mug. She's always picking on me, for some reason. I suppose I must look guilty.

'Because if you want to put your hand up now, it'll save an awful lot of embarrassment later.'

I look at Jack. He's staring straight at her, but his hand is speeding across the book at a rate of knots, composing his mini masterpiece. First law of not doing your homework – make eye contact with the teacher who's asking for it. That's what they do, scan the horizon for anyone who's not looking at them. Instant proof of guilt. It's obvious really, isn't it, but I was impressed when Jack pointed it out. Not that he ever has to use the technique. He's always done his homework.

'Good.' She turns her back a minute, writing something on the board.

I can see Jack's pen still scurrying across the book, a look of concentration knotting his eyebrows as he dashes off my twelve-line epic. I knew he wouldn't let me down.

'Okay, who's going to be the first to share their floral tribute with me and the rest of the class?' Tuna Chops' beady eyes roam the room on stalks, almost as obtrusive as her lips. They beam in on me as I dare to look down for a second, just to see if Jack has finished. I see him apply the final full stop.

'Ah, Luke. Yes. Off you go.'

I knew she'd pick on me. As she bends to sit down, Jack pushes the exercise book back at me.

'Come on, stand up and address the whole class,' Mrs Blythe says. 'Nice big voice, please. What's it called?'

I look down at the heading.

'"Hyacinth Wood", Mrs Blythe.'

'"Hyacinth Wood".' She sighs in mock anticipation. 'I can almost smell them from here. Take it away, please.'

Sarcasm is Mrs Blythe's stock in trade. She's very good at it, too.

I clear my throat.

'The sun arose across the hill
I lay beneath the tree
A butterfly just flitted by
And landed on my knee.'

Yousef Marn sniggers. Tuna Chops ignores him.

'When times are hard
When things get rough
I head for Hyacinth Wood
I forget about my homework and I think of something
good.'

Hmm. Mrs Blythe pushes her glasses back up her nose and looks out.

'Comments, anyone?'

People shuffle their papers and look away. I'm thinking, thanks, Jack. Thanks for nothing. Still at least it wasn't a big fat zero.

'Jack Duvall. What did you think of Luke's "Hyacinth Wood"?'

'Uninspiring, Mrs Blythe.'

'Wasn't it?' she agrees. 'What else?'

'He's used some rather trite rhymes, Miss. Wood – good. Tree – knee. He'd have done better to avoid the rhymes and concentrate on some more interesting images. Why say tree, for example, when he could have used "elm" or "oak" or something a little less . . .'

'Clichéd?' suggests Mrs Blythe.

'Exactly.'

'And how many lines do you think it was, Jack?'

Jack stops a moment and adds them up in his mind.

'I'd say eight.'

'Yes, I would too,' she agrees, staring at me. 'Do you have a problem with counting, Luke?'

'No, Mrs Blythe.'

'Well, would you like to read back over your poem and tell us how many lines you wrote?'

I look down at my book.

'Eight, Miss.'

'Yes.' She looks over the top of her specs at me this time. That's the advantage of glasses. They can be a useful weapon in classroom intimidation.

'And how many lines did I ask you to write, Luke Napier?'

'Twelve, Miss.'

'Yes, twelve. So in fact you've only done two-thirds of your homework, haven't you?'

'Yes, Mrs Blythe.'

'So you can do me a detention this evening, please. A whole hour. Not forty minutes. Is that understood?'

'Yes, Mrs Blythe.'

'Good. Now Jack, would you like to share your poem with us, please?'

Jack stands up. 'It's called, "Crushing the Petals to Release the Perfume".'

Mrs Blythe looks pleasantly surprised.

'Quite.'

'Thanks, pal.'

We're standing outside the science block. It's a couple of hours since the carnage that was 'Hyacinth Wood', but I'm still reeling from the sheer horror of it all.

'"Uninspiring, Mrs Blythe." "Trite rhymes, Mrs Blythe." "And I should know, Mrs Blythe, because I wrote it two minutes ago." And you obviously can't count.'

'Oh come on, Luke,' says Freya, setting about her apple as though she hasn't eaten all week. 'You didn't exactly give Jack a lot of time to compose a masterpiece now, did you?'

That's the trouble with Freya. She's always the voice of reason, always being fair to everyone.

'Wasn't as though you didn't have time to write anything yourself,' sniffs Jack huffily. 'I told you last night what the homework was. Anyway, why didn't you just play your trump card?'

'What trump card?'

'The sick brother in hospital,' he points out. 'It was worth a shot. I reckon it'd get you off detention at least.'

'Yeah, maybe you're right,' I say. 'I had other things on my mind last night in any case.'

'What things?'

Jack and Freya exchange glances.

'Like my mum. They've admitted her to Gospel Park.'

'Admitted her? I thought she already worked there?'

As I say, for a bright boy, Jack can sometimes be more than a little dim.

'Yes, she does work there. But she was ill yesterday and they've taken her in. All right? Got the picture now?'

I stomp off in a huff to make my point. That'll teach him to dash off total rubbish for my homework.

As I turn the corner, I almost walk slap bang into Mrs Blythe.

'Not looking where you're going, Luke.' It is an observation.

'Sorry, Mrs Blythe.'

'Perhaps you should concentrate a little harder on the

basics. Looking where you're going. Doing your home-work. Were you pleased with your poem this week, Luke?'

'No, Miss, it stank.'

For a moment I think she's going to smile.

'Didn't it? Still, at least you realise when you present something . . . something . . .'

I can see her grasping for a way to be tactful.

'Something totally pants?'

'Ah, yes. Totally pants. That just about covers it. You have a brain, Luke. A good one. You really ought to use it.'

'Yes, Miss.'

'And next time, don't rely on Jack Duvall to write your homework for you. His ability to count is "totally pants", too.'

She gives me another look, and I think I can see a smile play across her face. Tuna Chops? Smile? No, I must have imagined it.

'I don't know why,' she continues, 'but, against my better judgement, I'm going to let you off your detention this afternoon.'

'Thank you, Miss.'

'Don't let it happen again,' she throws over her shoulder as she turns away. Blimey, she is human after all.

Off she swishes in a blaze of brown corduroy, walking lopsidedly across the playing field, dodging kids and footballs as though she's negotiating a minefield. Ha, so she knew all along. Very crafty.

Freya suddenly appears in my line of vision. We've been friends since about Year Three, Freya and me, back in the days when boys weren't meant to be friends with girls. Now we're older and at secondary school, half the school thinks we're going out, and the other half doesn't care.

'Hey, what's wrong, Big Nose?'

She pushes a couple of strands of brown hair behind her ears, one of her more endearing habits. I can see Jack standing a few metres away, looking sheepish. Then she puts a friendly hand on my grey blazer.

'What's up with your mum?'

We sit on the railings and, as the grey clouds scud over our heads, I tell Jack and Freya all about Mum being ill. I don't tell them that I'm worried stupid or anything like that, but they're my mates, you know, I think they can work that out for themselves. A bit like old Tuna Chops and my flower poem. I tell them about Jesse too, and about 'staying the night at Jack's'.

'What are you going to do tonight?' Freya's always the practical one.

'Well, I'm going to see my mum obviously. She thinks they'll let her go home.'

'No, I mean, where are you going to stay if they don't let her out?'

I haven't really thought this far ahead. Much as I enjoyed staying up until two a.m. watching *Attack of the Giant Killer Bees From Mars* on the movie channel, I don't really want another night home alone. To be honest, I was a little freaked out by the time I got into bed. I notice it's starting to rain now and I begin to think about Mum lying in her hospital bed, probably bored stupid and desperately trying to escape. I wonder how Jesse is too. The prat.

'Blimey – sixty-six per cent of one family in hospital at the same time,' says Jack, maths whizz-kid, sucking in sharply. 'You'd better watch yourself, Luke. It could be an ancient Egyptian curse.'

'Considering you can't tell the difference between an eight-line poem and a twelve-line poem, that's quite an impressive calculation,' I tell him.

'Why don't you sleep at mine if your mum is still in hospital?' he continues, ignoring me. 'My mum won't mind. I'll text her now.'

He gets his mobile phone out. It looks like a real dud, the kind of phone you'd get free with a few tokens off the back of a cornflake packet, but, as Jack always points out, at least it works and no one in their right mind would ever want to nick it. I had a snazzy Nokia that some bunch of no-marks lifted from me in the park before I'd even had a chance to explore its fifty-three different functions. Now I have a mobile so ordinary that I leave it at home most of the time (including today when I could really use it). Still, it's not as sad as Jack's.

'What about your detention?' says Freya. 'I know you wheedled your way out of Blythe's but I thought you got logged this morning for being late?'

'Ah,' I say. 'Yes. True.'

'Okay, pass me the chitty,' she says.

I rummage in my pocket and dig out the crumpled detention form I'd forgotten about.

'*Napier, 10N,*' reads Freya. 'Just as I thought. Okay, I'll do your detention for you. You owe me one.'

'What? How?'

'Duh,' she says. 'It's never the same prefect who does detention and they have no idea who we are. They only write your surname and class down. So tonight, Freya Napier is in detention and you can go and see your mum at the hozzie.'

'You'd do that for me?' I say.

'Once,' says Freya. 'I'll do it once. If you don't haul your bony carcass out of bed tomorrow, boy, you can do your own detention.'

Jack's phone beeps.

'We're on,' he says. 'You can stay at mine tonight.'

'What about Jesse?' I say. 'He should be home tonight.'

'Bring him too,' says Jack. 'Mum won't mind.'

'Oh cheers,' I say. 'Didn't fancy another night home alone.'

To tell the truth, I've eaten the last pizza anyway.

chapter six

When I arrive at the hospital, there's Jesse perched on the end of Mum's bed like some kind of chirpy pet, his head nodding away, looking all perky and reading another stupid football magazine. Mum, on the other hand, is propped up on a pillow, looking even greyer than last time. There are dark rings under her eyes, and she holds me for a moment too long as we hug, so I know that things still aren't right.

'I missed school today.' Jesse looks up, pleased with himself.

'Yeah, well, you'll have to catch up when you get back, bird-brain, won't you?' I say.

'C'mon boys,' says Mum. 'Let's not have any arguments. Not while I'm in here. Feeling like this.'

'Like what?' says Jesse. He's lobbing grapes into his mouth like they're Maltesers.

'Did the doctor say anything today?' I ask.

Mum sighs.

'No, just took lots of blood. Tests and more tests. I feel like a pin cushion.' She rubs her arm inside her elbow, and I can see the little tell-tale red pricks.

'Can you run out of blood?' says Jesse. He's throwing grapes in the air now and trying to catch them in his open mouth. The grapes are going all over the floor.

'Why don't you go and get yourself some chocolate from that machine downstairs, Jesse?' says Mum. 'Here, take some money from my purse . . .'

He's already scrabbling about in Mum's purse looking for change, he doesn't need asking twice, and then he's off down the ward like he's heading for goal. I can tell Mum wants a word with me on my own. She grabs hold of my hand.

'Look, love,' she says, biting her lip nervously, 'I may be in here a bit longer than I expected.'

'What? How long? You said you thought you'd be home tonight.'

'Yes, I know I did,' says Mum. 'But they don't want to let me out until they know what it is.' She passes a hand over my forehead now, gently pushing back a lock of my hair. It flops back again immediately. 'They won't know until they get the test results back. And that takes time, it'll be a couple of days.'

'A couple of days? What are we supposed to do?'

'It's the NHS, you know,' says Mum. 'It's not geared up to instant results.'

She squeezes my hand tighter.

'You're going to have to be very grown-up about this, Luke,' she says, 'for Jesse's sake, as well as for mine. I know it's not ideal, but remember he's younger than you. He needs looking after.'

'By who?' I say. 'Not by you. You're stuck in here.'

I feel cheated, let down. Mum gets ill and I get stuck with Jesse. Where's the fairness in that?

'I can't take care of him properly while I'm in here. So . . . I've arranged for someone to come and look after you both,' says Mum.

'I don't need looking after! I'm nearly fifteen.'

'You may not think you need looking after now,' says Mum, speaking slowly and patiently in a quiet voice to counteract my increase in volume, 'but you do.'

'Who is it?' I ask, picking at her bedspread. I'm so wound up by this I don't even want to look at her. 'Who are you sending to babysit us?'

'She's called Mrs McLafferty. She's the auntie of a friend of Mia,' says Mum. 'She can start tomorrow, so you'll need to spend another night with Jack.'

'You don't even know her,' I say. 'How do you know she's not some kookie old pervert?'

'She's not,' says Mum. 'Mia knows her and says she's a lovely lady. Older lady,' she adds quietly.

I give Mum one of my defiant looks.

'Older? What – how old?'

'I don't know, Luke,' says Mum. Her voice sounds tired now. 'Younger than the Queen, older than Marge Simpson. How's that? I've only spoken to her on the phone. She sounds . . . fine.'

'Fine,' I say with all the sarcasm I can muster. 'That's probably what they said about Attila the Hun.'

'You know what the alternative is, don't you?' says Mum. 'Social services. Fostering. It's messy. You and Jesse may get split up and that's the last thing I want right now.'

'I could go and live with Jack,' I say. But even as I say this, I'm thinking of that horrible mattress and I know that's not going to happen.

'No you couldn't. They haven't got the space. Oh, the odd sleepover is fine, but . . . I just don't know how long I'm going to be in here, love,' says Mum. She puts her hand back up to touch my face again, but this time I push it away.

'I want you and Jesse in our house – your house,' Mum explains. Her voice is rising and I can hear she's getting a bit teary. 'So I know where you are. So you're sleeping in your own beds and going to your own school and you're there when I come home . . .' Just then, Sister Calder is passing the bed. She looks over towards us. She chooses her moments.

'Everything all right here?' she asks, glancing down at Mum's clipboard that she's picked up from the foot of the bed.

I mumble yes, and Mum turns her head to the side so that Sister can't see she's crying.

'Luke, can I have a quick word?' Sister says. 'In private. In my office.'

Oh, here we go, I think. She's just another Mrs Halloran.

I can hear the supper trolley arriving as we head off down the ward. It smells like school dinners, only it's possibly worse. Presumably it all comes from the same slop factory.

'Take a seat,' says Sister Calder. There's a chart on the wall and a washbasin in the corner. She's washing her hands under a big *BEAT MRSA – WASH YOUR HANDS* poster. I sit down quietly.

'Your mother isn't very well, Luke,' says Sister. She's scrubbing away between her fingers as she speaks.

'What is it? What's wrong with her?'

'Oh, it's too early to say.' She is pulling green paper towels from a dispenser to dry her hands. 'But it looks as though she won't be going home for a while yet. Now, I know you don't have a dad around, and I know it's not ideal, but your mum has spent most of today worrying about you and your brother and trying to sort something out so you can both carry on living at home.

I think you're going to have to trust her on this one, Luke. If your mother's worrying about you and your brother, she's not going to get any better, is she? All that energy that could be spent recovering . . . well, it's wasting away fretting about the two of you.'

She fixes me with her deep brown eyes.

'She needs her rest, Luke.'

I can see her point here.

'Yes, I know,' I say.

'So no scenes, eh? No fusses? The best thing you can do is stay cheerful and look after your brother. That's the best way to help your mum get better, quicker.'

There's a huge crash from outside. Sister stands up and looks over my shoulder through the glass panel in the door.

'Ah, talk of the devil,' she says. 'Here's your brother now. Does he like baked beans?' she asks me.

'Not much. Why?'

'He's had a small collision with the supper trolley,' says Sister Calder as she opens the door. 'Seems he's been bathing in them.'

chapter seven

That's how Mrs McLafferty comes into our world. The next day, before we've had time to turn our lives into a *Lord of the Flies* meets *Big Brother* type experiment, she just turns up on the doorstep with an old battered green suitcase and a fluffy grey hat that must date back to the war. The Boer War, probably. When I open the door, and I see her standing there, things don't quite connect at first.

She's all of four feet ten inches tall, leering out from behind her very scary red lipstick. So red I can't help wondering what animals she's been slaughtering. You can't tell how old Mrs McLafferty is, she has a certain Sphinx-like quality about her. She could be over a hundred for all I know.

'Luke?' she enquires with a big question mark at the end, like she doesn't know. Her pencilled-in luminous ginger eyebrows rise an inch or two to emphasise the query.

'Yes?' Two can play at that game. I try to raise my eyebrows too, but I can tell I'm failing miserably.

'The name's McLafferty, Mrs McLafferty. But you can call me Mrs M.'

Her soft Irish accent rises and falls, lulling me into a false sense of security.

'I'm here to look after you while your mammy's in hospital,' she explains, roughly shoving the door open as she breezes past.

'Now, perhaps you'd like to show me up to my room,' she declares, marching up the stairs. 'Don't forget my case now. Nothing for a big strong boy like you.'

I have no idea what she's got in that case but it feels like a ton of bricks.

As we get to the landing, Jesse sticks his head out of his room.

'Hello, young man,' she says matter-of-factly. For a moment I think she's going to shake his hand, but she just pushes her bosoms back into position and barges past.

I still have no idea where she is heading. We only have three bedrooms – mine, Mum's and Jesse's. I suppose I could direct Mrs M towards the sofa.

As if she can read my mind, she opens the door to Mum's room.

'This looks like me,' she says, waltzing in and looking at the furniture with disdain, running a finger along

Mum's dressing table to check for any tell-tale sign of dust. 'No ensuite, I suppose?'

'Sweets? Where?' Jesse can't resist a quick look.

'Not sweets,' she explains. 'An ensuite bathroom. It's a bedroom with a bathroom attached.'

'We only have one bathroom,' I tell her.

'Then we'll just have to share, won't we?' she says, waggling her head from side to side. I wonder if she's trying to take the mick.

'What are you doing in Mum's room?' asks Jesse.

'I'm Mrs McLafferty,' she explains, grabbing Jesse's hands in that way that grown-ups do when they want to talk to you like you're still a toddler. 'I'm here to look after you boys while your poor sick mammy languishes in a hospital bed, worried half to death by the two of yous, no doubt, and the thought of what you're getting up to in her absence.'

We should be so lucky, I think. Jesse looks aghast. Mum had told him we were getting someone to look after us but the reality has clearly knocked him for six.

'Now you,' she points at me, 'can put my case on the chair – Luke, isn't it? – and you,' she points at Jesse, 'can go and put the kettle on. What's your name?'

She can't get her head round 'Jesse'.

'But sure, it's a girl's name, isn't it?' she says scowling and turning up her nose. 'Jesse . . .'

'No, it's not,' says Jesse. 'It's my name. And what about Jesse James? He wasn't a girl.'

'Jesse James?' Mrs M rolls her eyes up to the sky. 'Your mother never went and named you after a notorious outlaw. Jeez, I've heard it all now.'

She sits her lumpy little frame down on Mum's cream bedspread. Mum saw it in some swanky catalogue months ago and saved up for ages. We're not allowed to go anywhere near it, let alone touch it. Somehow it doesn't seem right, this stranger smoothing Mum's cream bedspread down with her hand as she plonks her bum on the bed.

'Ow, that's hard,' she says, squinting her eyes up in mock pain. 'I'll never get a wink on a tough old bed like that.'

'Mum says it's the best bed in the world,' I tell her. 'She always says that.'

'Well, any port in a storm, I suppose,' she says, ignoring me and looking round the room. She's pricing everything up in her mind's eye, I can tell.

'What's your name again?' asks Jesse.

'Mrs McLafferty, but you can call me Mrs M,' she says. 'Everyone does. And I don't know what you're gawping at, Jesse,' she spits his name out venomously, 'have you not got that kettle on yet?'

'That's better,' says Mrs M. She's hunched over a cup of

tea in the kitchen, alternately blowing into her mug and slurping enthusiastically.

'Mind you, I'll never get used to these mugs. I never drink out of mugs. Are you sure your mother hasn't a cup and saucer stashed away somewhere?'

Jesse and I shake our heads.

'No?' She looks crestfallen. 'Well, I don't suppose either of you boys knows where I'd lay hands on a cigarette now, do you?' She shrinks her nose up in disdain. 'What's a cup of tea without a cigarette?'

'Smoking kills,' says Jesse, dunking his fifth Jaffa cake. 'We did it at school.'

'Ah, did you now?' says Mrs M, confiscating the rest of the Jaffa cakes and putting them back in the biscuit tin. 'Well, I'd kill for a puff right now, I would. Are you sure there's not a packet lying around somewhere? Some secret stash . . .'

She looks at me innocently.

'Just one ciggie. No questions asked.'

'I don't smoke,' I say. 'It's a disgusting habit.'

Mrs M starts rummaging in her fake leather handbag now, with the 'leather' peeling off in places. She shoves her head right into the bag as though she's being devoured.

'Now where was it . . .'

She scrabbles around a bit more and eventually resurfaces, triumphant, with a beaten-up-looking cigarette held aloft between two fingers.

'Ha!'

She holds it up closely to her eyes, snaps the filter tip off at one end, and sticks the other end in her mouth. Then she lights it, breathing the smoke in deeply, and shutting her eyes in pleasure.

'Aren't they more dangerous without the ends on?' asks Jesse, picking up the filter tip to examine it at closer quarters.

'Possibly,' says Mrs M, drinking in the smoke, 'but these mild ones have got no flavour with the filters.' Taking another gulp of tea, Mrs M turns to face me.

'Now, what do you want for your tea tonight?'

I shrug my shoulders.

'Don't mind. Anything. We like pizza.'

'Pizza!' She screws her nose up in disgust, and takes another drag on her fag.

'Sure, it's nothing but a bit of old dough with a smear of ketchup on the top. Where's the nutrition in that? No, while I'm here it's proper healthy meals for growing boys like you.'

She drops the fag end in her mug and it goes out with a sizzle and a little puff of smoke like a damp squib.

'Not much in here,' she says, rooting through the fridge and tutting away to herself. 'I'm heading off up to the shops now – your mother's given me some money. I'll get you some nice liver for your tea.'

She says it like it's a treat.

As the door slams shut, I look across at Jesse. He looks at me.

'Liver,' he says. 'I don't like the sound of that.'

'No,' I agree. 'I'm not so keen on her either. She seems to have taken over the whole house and she's only been here half an hour.' I shake my head. 'She's got to go.'

chapter eight

'Orange. She sounds like a complete nightmare,' says Freya as she bites into the Revel. We're sitting on the top of a mound (you could hardly call it a hill) in Edgerley Park, just round the corner from Freya's house. It's a Saturday morning bathed in sunshine, the whole weekend stretching ahead, and we're discussing Mrs M and playing 'I'll Name That Revel' at the same time. It's our favourite game. All you need is a packet of Revels, and you take one out at a time – no peeking in the bag first – then guess what it is just by looking at it before you put it in your mouth.

'She treats the place like it's her own home,' I say. 'First she moves into Mum's room, then she starts bossing us around, and now she's started wearing Mum's clothes. Caramel.'

The caramels tend to be easier to spot on account of their slightly irregular shape. I bite in and hold the evidence up to Freya, who nods to recognise I've got another right.

'You sound like Angela moaning about me.' Angela's her mum. 'Mind you, wearing your mum's clothes is a bit creepy,' says Freya sympathetically.

'I know. It started with the odd cardigan and I just assumed she was cold – but now she's wearing her dressing gown and nightie – and she had one of Mum's skirts on the other day.'

'What you need,' Freya says, delving back into the Revels, 'is a concerted plan of attack to get rid of the old bag. But you'll have to get Jesse on side or it's doomed to failure. Malteser.'

The Maltesers are dead easy to spot: they're bigger and lighter than the others. It's the orange and coffee creams that can catch you out. We both love the orange ones and hate the coffee creams, so it's a bit like playing Russian Roulette with chocolates. There's nothing more distressing than thinking you've got a juicy orange cream and then biting in to discover it's actually the revolting coffee filth.

'Yes, but say we do manage to drive her away,' I point out, 'who's going to look after us once she's gone? They'll probably send social services round.'

'Oh yes, I hadn't thought of that,' Freya agrees. 'Wait a minute, what about your dad?'

'My dad? You *are* kidding? All I know is he's up in

Scotland somewhere, living a new life with a new family and new friends for all I know. Let's not open that particular can of worms.'

'Looks like you're stuck with Mrs M for a bit longer, then,' says Freya. 'Mmm, chocolate.'

She bites into a flying-saucer-shaped Revel, a total gift in this game.

'How is your mum? Is she getting any better? You never talk about it at school.'

I've been asked this question a lot lately and it's the one I'm beginning to dread. Simply because Mum's been in hospital for a few weeks now and it seems we're no closer to finding out what's actually the matter with her. I normally say, 'Yeah, she's on the mend,' and change the subject or just fudge an answer, but this is Freya and I don't want to fob off one of my best mates. I've only got two after all.

'Well, they've done more tests this week, but the doctors still don't know what it is.' I tell her what I've been told. 'In the meantime, we have Nanzilla driving us mental. I can't take much more of her,' I moan. 'She leaves ash-trays all round the house, her cooking is disgusting, and she's always trying to pack us off to bed early so she can get stuck into the whisky she carries round in a hip flask in her handbag.'

'Hardly Mary Poppins material,' Freya observes. 'Why don't you try poisoning her?'

'What, like she's trying to poison us with her liver casserole and her grisly gammon steaks? She won't let us anywhere near the kitchen. I can't remember the last time I had a decent pizza. Besides, you can't buy arsenic over the counter at Boots, in case you hadn't noticed.'

'Does Jesse get on with her?' Freya's mind is running off at a tangent now.

'Oh, you know what he's like. She hardly crosses his radar except when his footie kit isn't ready when he needs it, or if she's having a go at him for getting it caked in mud. Mum never seemed to care.'

We've finished the Revels now, and Freya screws up the bag and lobs it towards the bin. She misses, tuts, and has to hoist herself off her elbows to go and pick up the bag and put it into the bin from point-blank range.

'Why don't you just tell your mum that Mrs M isn't all she's cracked up to be? That she's a lazy good-for-nothing old boozer who's past her sell-by date?'

'Then Mum will start worrying about who's going to look after us. And that's not exactly going to help her get better, is it?'

'Good point,' says Freya, lying down on her stomach. 'Hey, Luke, you know that phrase, "You can fool all of the people some of the time, some of the people all of the time . . ."'

'Yes, ". . . but not all of the people all of time". What's that got to do with it?' I ask.

'What I mean is, she's bound to get caught out sooner or later, isn't she?'

Freya turns on to her back and lies with her head towards the sun, shielding her face from the force of its glare with the back of her hand. I can tell she's thinking hard – I can practically hear her brain working.

'Well, you just have to make sure she's not fooling everyone . . .'

'Explain.'

'Who told your mum about Mrs M?'

'Erm, it was Mia.'

Freya's on her feet, looking triumphant. 'Exactly! Mia! All you have to do is get Mia round and show her what a disaster Mrs M is. Then *she* can sort out getting rid of her. End of problem.'

Well, I have to admit, it's better than her poison plot.

'Have you left Jesse home alone with Mrs M?' asks Freya.

'Only for an hour or two. He's washing his footie kit. She reckons she'd done it, but it wasn't up to Jesse's exacting standards. He likes it to look pristine and sparkling red and white when he walks on the pitch.'

'What, so it contrasts nicely with the mud-caked disaster area that walks off at the end, you mean?'

'That's if he's lucky enough to walk off after ninety minutes,' I say. 'It's normally worth betting he'll be stretchered off before the end. The trouble with Jesse is, he's fearless. He'll go after every ball, get stuck into every tackle, take on any player, even if it means doing himself damage in the process. You know who coaches them? Mr Rubinstein.'

Freya feigns horror.

'Not Rottweiler Rubinstein.'

'One and the same. Well, he says that what Jesse lacks in talent he makes up for in the way of bravery, but I reckon it's just stupidity. After all, self-preservation is one of the guiding principles of human nature. If cavemen had gone running after wild bears like total freaks, the human race would have been wiped out years ago.'

Suddenly I glance at my watch and jump up.

'Oh shit, it's kick-off in twenty minutes.'

'Kick-off?' says Freya. 'Since when did you bother yourself about kick-off? Don't pretend you're interested in football.'

'I'm not,' I admit, 'but Jesse got a bit upset the other day because Mum can't go and watch him play, so she made me promise I'd go instead.'

'Well, I can think of worse ways to spend a couple of hours,' says Freya.

'Like what? Dusting Mrs M's precious collection of chipped ornaments?'

I stand up and start brushing bits of grass and dirt

off my jeans. 'Jesse's even managed to persuade Jack to come along.'

'Jack!' says Freya with a wry smile. 'He's about as interested in football as he is in knitting. Or cooking . . .'

True, Jack's not the world's greatest chef. In fact, I've only ever had one meal he tried to cook for me. Okay, I use the term 'meal' loosely. It was actually an omelette. Well, he said it was an omelette. I was convinced it was an oddment from the local latex factory. I swear it bounced a good twelve centimetres when he flopped it on to my plate.

'Who knows?' I laugh. 'Maybe we'll get a liking for it today. Fancy coming along?'

'Sorry, I'm, er . . . washing the goldfish bowl . . . no, the car . . . oh, my hair . . .' Freya flounders. This isn't like her. She can normally come up with a diamond excuse without batting an eyelid.

'They can all wait,' I tell her. 'You said you could think of worse ways to spend a couple of hours. You're coming too.'

As she stands up I move across and take a very unsubtle sniff at her hair.

'Although on second thoughts . . . when *was* the last time you washed your hair?'

chapter nine

'Oh, I see you got roped into this torture too,' says Jack to Freya. He's standing on the touchline by one of the goalposts, clapping his hands against his sides. He's wearing a thick, fleece-lined fur-trimmed parka zipped up to his chin with his 1980s Dr Who scarf wrapped round his neck three times (it's still hanging down to his ankles). He's stamping his feet and clapping his arms about himself in that crazy way people do when they're waiting for a bus at the South Pole.

'I thought we were watching a football match,' says Freya.

'I am,' says Jack. 'Don't know about you.'

'Looks like you're going on a polar expedition,' she says. 'Do you think you've wrapped up warm enough?'

Jack gives her the finger.

'Take the hood off, Jack,' I tell him. 'It's scorchio.

You look a prat dressed like that.'

It's only April but the sun is beating down like it's August. Jack's body thermostat must have blown a fuse. Reluctantly, he pulls back the hood.

'It's always cold at football matches,' he grumbles. 'Last time I went to a football match, I nearly caught pneumonia.'

'Oh yeah, and when exactly was that, Jack?' asks Freya.

'Erm, let me see . . .' Jack starts calculating in earnest. 'It must have been January, about five years ago.'

'Exactly,' I say. 'There's been a whole lot of global warming going on since then, Jack. And this is April. Just take the coat off and stop drawing attention to yourself.'

If there's one thing that never fails to amaze me about Jesse, it's his powers of persuasion. He can get a 'yes' out of people when you know darn well the answer should be 'no'. 'Mum, can I stay up late and watch the football?' 'Sir, can I leave a little early to visit my mum in hospital?' I can't believe he's actually managed to get Jack to agree to come to this poxy match, but he has. Jack knows even less about football than I do.

The teams start trooping out on to the pitch. It's Cawlsham College in the blue-and-white hooped shirts, and we're in red-and-white stripes. Jesse's waving to us as he runs on and manages to tread on Shav's ankles in front of him. Shav's the star striker and he's not happy that a pathetic little upstart like Jesse is hogging the limelight, so he turns and punches him, fake-friendly, if you know what I mean. Jesse takes it as a bit of pre-match camaraderie and rubs his shoulder in good heart, but I can tell it must have hurt.

'How long do these matches last?' asks Jack. 'I'm sure I've got some geography homework that requires my urgent attention.'

'Shut up and watch,' I say. 'If I can do this, so can you. And it's not due till Tuesday anyway.'

'It's ninety minutes,' says Freya. 'That's forty-five each way. Do you want me to explain the off-side rule to you both now or later?'

We stare at her, open-mouthed, as she launches into a very thorough explanation.

'Come on, guys,' she smiles. 'This is the twenty-first century. Girls can like football, you know.'

'You never let on,' I accuse.

'You never asked.' Freya cups her hands together and screams, 'Come on, Joan of Arc! Come on, you reds!' very professionally.

'School football's not exactly my scene,' she adds. 'I'm normally more of a Premiership girl. But in for a penny, I s'pose . . .'

'I brought my rattle,' says Jack. From under his parka, he produces this huge wooden football rattle with a flourish. It looks like it's about a hundred years old and there's a distinct possibility of dry rot round the joints.

'Give it a whirl, then,' says Freya, sniggering.

Jack lifts the rattle slowly (it's obviously no featherweight) and cranks it round his head a couple of times. The effect is instantaneous: it gives off the most earth-shattering almighty racket I've ever heard in my life. It's as loud as a jumbo jet taking off just above our heads. A flock of seagulls that has been hanging out on the other side of the park take flight, never to return, and everyone, including all the players, turns and looks in our direction.

'It's quite loud, isn't it?' says Jack.

'Stop it now,' says Freya, who's not keen on all the attention we're attracting. Come to think of it, nor is Jack. His face has lit up like a thousand-watt bulb, and it's glowing infra-red.

'Where'd you get that from?' asks Jesse as he runs over to Jack. He's been sent by his team-mates to investigate the god-awful, ear-drum-shattering noise that came from our direction.

'It's my grandad's,' says Jack. 'I borrowed it from him. He always used to take it when he went to watch a match. He reckoned it brought them good luck.'

'Whatever,' says Jesse. 'Anyway, Callum – he's the captain – he says it's going to be a bit off-putting for the players if you start rattling that thing about. And anyway, they're banned. So Callum says, can you shut it please?'

'Look,' I say, wading in, 'We've come to support you. Make some noise. Isn't that what it's all about? Talk about ungrateful.'

'Come on, you reds,' shouts Freya again, at the top of her voice.

'He says you can shout out, if you like,' says Jesse, looking at Freya. 'That's all right. But nothing rude. No swearing. And definitely no rattling. Please?'

'No swearing?' Freya is outraged. 'Has he ever been to a football match? This isn't a dress rehearsal for *The Sound of Music*, you know!'

'Jesse!' yells Mr Rubinstein. 'Over here. Now!' It's not hard to see why he came to be called Rottweiler. It's no wonder Jesse is always so serious about the team – I'd be terrified of getting on the wrong side of him. The story goes that he used to play for a Premiership side a few years back – I think it was Aston Villa – until someone chopped him down one Saturday and he took a bite out of their ear in retaliation. According to the legend that circulated at school, Rottweiler never made it back into the first team again, and ended up enrolling at teachers' training college at the end of the season. Jesse runs back to join his team-mates, who largely seem to ignore him. They're about to kick off. The whistle blows.

'Do you want me to explain the off-side rule again?' says Freya.

'No, you're all right,' says Jack. 'It doesn't seem

right, running in the opposite direction to the play, does it? Are you sure you've got it right?'

What I never understand about football is all that hanging around. There are twenty-two people on the pitch – okay, twenty-three if you count the ref – and just that one little ball. And only one player at a time has the ball, right? So how dull is that for the others? Whenever I point this out to Jesse, he always goes on about everyone being focussed on the game, but I don't buy that. They must be bored witless.

Freya reckons it's a fairly even first half with Cawlsham having the upper hand – just. So, as the score is nil-nil, I suppose we're doing okay. Jesse's been running around a lot and he's touched the ball about six times and fallen over three times, which is fairly good going for him. There's still a fair bit of mud about, despite the sunshine, so he's got his usual chocolate frosting.

'When are you next going to see your mum, Big Nose?' asks Freya.

'Later this afternoon,' I say. 'Got to go to the library for that World War II project in history, then I'll bike over this afternoon. Why?'

'Oh, well send her my love,' says Freya. 'My mum and I might pop down and see her next week.'

'Yeah, that's cool,' I say. 'I'm sure she'd like to see you both. It gets really boring for her in hospital.'

'Talking of boring . . .' Jack's pulling on his parka.

'You're not going till the fat lady sings,' I say, pointing at Jack.

'She's got a sore throat. She's not singing today,' he says sulkily. He looks over at the team, who are sucking away on their orange segments as if they hold the key to eternal youth – or at least the Inter-County Schools Under-16s Challenge.

'Do you think they've got any spare oranges? I'm quite thirsty.'

Freya produces a bottle of water from her bag which she hands to Jack. He starts swigging away in big noisy gulps so I suppose that means he's here for the second half. The whistle blows, and they're off again.

This half, it looks like Rottweiler Rubinstein has given our lot a bit of a pep talk. Jesse's playing midfield and he actually manages to squeeze in a couple of decent tackles, so we shout some encouragement and cheer a bit, and next thing we know is he's booting the ball up the wing to Shav who curves it round one dopey-looking defender, puts on a bit of a spurt to get past him, then hooks it over the goalie's head and into the back of the net.

One-nil. We all cheer a bit. Jack gets out his rattle, but Freya gives him such a dirty look that he puts it away again. A couple of other Joan of Arc dads are shouting encouragement like it's a proper football match and it really matters. Jesse's got a big cheesy grin on his face. Shav claps him on the back to acknowledge his part in the goal.

The rest of the game is almost quite exciting. Cawlsham actually put a bit more effort in and start to hit back, and Freya and Jack and I start calling out and cheering Jesse on (well, okay, Freya does most of the shouting and the odd bit of swearing). They get a couple of shots at goal, but they don't score, then Rottweiler starts waving his arms about and screaming, telling them 'to get back and defend their lead' (only there's quite a bit more swearing in there too). This has the opposite effect, of course, and Joan of Arc start making some serious inroads into the Cawlsham defence. Mark Chetley kicks the ball across the box and Raul, one of our best defenders, so I have no idea what he's doing at that end of the field, but anyway, he hurls his head into its path and bam! It's up in the corner of the net and it's two-nil. Jack can't resist giving the rattle a good CLACK-CLACK-CLACK and he screams, 'See I told you it was lucky' over the din, and Freya and I dance around a bit and generally get into the swing of things. Five minutes later, the game's over and we're heading for home.

chapter ten

On the way home, we stop for some chips. I'd managed to get some lunch money out of Mrs M in the morning, which is a cause for celebration as she's very tight with the housekeeping. So we're sharing a massive portion of chips and a greasy-looking saveloy (Jesse's idea) as we walk up Baron's Hill together. Jesse's still wearing his kit and he's caked in mud. The Turkish bloke in the chip shop won't let him in, so I have to select his saveloy for him.

'Looks a bit small,' he whinges when I hand it over.

'You've got potential,' Freya is saying to Jesse, waving a chip to emphasise her point as she walks part of the way home with us. Jack scarpered as soon as the final whistle rang, afraid Rottweiler was going to try and confiscate his rattle.

'Do you think so?' says Jesse. 'I'm the youngest in the team so I know I'm not as fast as the rest.'

'Speed isn't your problem,' says Freya. 'You have acceleration anyway. No, you just need to anticipate better. It's all up here.' She taps the side of her head with her finger. 'You've got to know what the opposition is thinking, where he's going to play the ball next. I can help you if you like.'

'Really?' says Jesse. 'I know Duane Mulholland thinks he should be on the team, not me. He's bigger and faster than me, so I need all the help I can get.'

'Size and speed aren't everything,' says Freya, nicking another chip. 'Meet me after school on Monday up at the rec. Bring your kit – I'll supply the ball.'

She waves goodbye to us both as she peels off up Weybridge Avenue.

As we open the door, we hear the unmistakable sound of Mrs M warbling away as she vacuums the living room. It's an old Irish song, 'The Rose of Tralee', and her thin wispy voice goes all quivery when she hit the high notes.

'The pale moon was rising above the green mountains,
The sun was declining beneath the blue sea . . .'

To be fair, the hoover probably isn't the best accompaniment, but she's singing her heart out just the same.

'Ah, boys,' she says, turning to face us. 'God only knows why your mother has these draughty old wooden boards when she could have a nice Axminster.

They're a bugger to hoover, if you'll pardon my French.'

Mrs M stops dead as she takes in Jesse in his muddy kit.

'Glory be, look at the state of yous, flaking your mud all over my nice clean floor. Get out now.' She adds under her breath, 'And I've just done in here, too.'

She heads for the kitchen and comes back with a few sheets of newspaper for Jesse to stand on and a plastic carrier bag.

'Clothes in there,' she says, holding the carrier out to him, 'and then up to the shower with you.'

'I'm not stripping naked in front of you,' says Jesse indignantly. By now, he's mastered the fine art of being rude to Mrs M without actually offending her, mainly because he's worked out she has a soft spot for him. I'd never dare to be rude – for one thing, she blatantly doesn't like me, and for another, once the floodgates are opened, who knows what's going to happen next?

'Luke, will you nip upstairs and grab your brother's dressing gown,' says Mrs M, 'though Lord knows why he's making all this fuss. Do you think I've never seen a boy naked before?'

'I don't care,' says Jesse. 'You're not seeing me naked. Pervert.'

'Well, don't you go moving off that paper,' says Mrs M wagging a finger at him in exasperation, 'or I'll come and scrub the mud off you myself with a big bristly brush. You should have a shower straight after you've finished playing football, not when you get home. Sure, it's all caked in everywhere.'

I go upstairs and grab Jesse's dressing gown from his room and chuck it at him downstairs.

'Cheers,' he moans. 'Now can I have some privacy please?'

As I go into the kitchen, Mrs M announces, 'I've had the hospital on the phone this afternoon, Luke.'

'The hospital?' I say.

'Yes, it seems your mammy's not been feeling too good today. She had a bad night. So they said it's best not to go in this weekend, to let her rest for a couple of days. You can call her tomorrow and see how she's feeling.'

'Jesse will be disappointed,' I say. 'He was looking forward to telling her about the match. They're into the semi-finals.'

'Oh, is that right?' says Mrs M. I might as well have told her the moon is made of blue cheese – she hasn't a clue what I'm on about.

'The semis, eh? Well, isn't that grand?' she goes on. 'And I've taken one of my lovely casseroles out of the freezer for later this evening.'

Jesse is feeling really low tonight, I can tell, and it isn't just Mrs M's casserole that's to blame. I challenge him to his favourite game in the world, Cluedo, and we're playing at the kitchen table. We used to play all our board games here with Mum. She was never a big fan of Cluedo, mainly because Jesse used to get paranoid that either Mum or I was going to win, and so he'd just guess any old rubbish, ages before he'd worked it out properly. Then, when he checked and discovered he was wrong, he'd get in a big strop and stomp off. End of game. Typical Jesse.

We've managed to persuade Mrs M to join in too, just to make up the numbers, though she doesn't have any idea what's going on in the game. But as Jesse throws the dice and wanders from room to room, picking up bits of lead piping, the candlestick and some wool (we lost the original rope ages ago and improvised with some yarn from Mum's sewing box), I can see he's getting more and more upset. The telly is on in the corner and Mrs M is obviously more interested in *Harry Hill's TV Burp* than the game. I'm just moving Colonel Mustard off to the conservatory for a bit of questioning when I hear Jesse sniff and I can see a tear drip off his nose and splash on to Professor Plum. Suddenly he belts upstairs. Mrs M is chortling at some daft sketch and doesn't even notice we've both left the room.

Upstairs I knock on Jesse's door and go in, not bothering to wait for a reply. He'd probably just tell me to get lost, or something ruder, I figure, so I may as well take my chances.

'What's up with you?' I ask. 'Come on, spill.'

Jesse is lying face down on his bed.

'Nothing,' he says.

'Yeah, like you've had your best day's footie ever, you're as happy as a kid's TV presenter all afternoon, and you're blubbing like a big baby by the evening,' I say. 'So, come on. Tell me what's wrong.'

'It's Mum,' he says. 'I miss her. I just wanted to tell her about the match tonight, you know. So I could share it with her.'

'Look,' I reply, 'we'll go tomorrow, whatever they say. It's only one day. She's bound to be better by tomorrow. They can't stop us, and she'll want to see us anyway. She'll even want to hear about you and your tedious little match.'

He smiles a bit at that. I pull a pile of tissues out of the box.

'I really miss her,' he says again, his eyes starting to leak more tears. 'It's been weeks now, and she doesn't seem to get any better. In fact, she's getting worse.'

'Crap, Jesse,' I tell him. 'She's got to get worse before she gets better. That's what she told us. That's how it works sometimes. She should know, Jesse. She's a nurse.'

'Yeah I s'pose,' he grunts through the tears.

'I know so,' I say with confidence. Only I don't. I'm

just putting on a brave face for him, really. It's what Freya calls the Power of Positive Thinking. The worst thing is, I know Jesse's right. Mum isn't getting any better. Last time we went in, we even had to help prop her up in bed so she could sit and chat to us. But even chatting seems to wear her out now.

'She's having a bad day,' Sister Calder had said on Friday when we last saw her. Mum seemed to have an awful lot of nasty pills to swallow when the drugs trolley came round – some were huge – and it took her ages to get them all down.

'We'll go tomorrow, for sure,' I say again, brightly. 'But don't say anything about the old bag downstairs,' I warn. 'I don't think we should go upsetting Mum. Anyway, I've got a plan for getting rid of her.'

'Have you?' Jesse looks more cheerful already. 'What is it?'

'All in good time,' I say. 'Want to watch some telly now?'

'Yeah, all right,' he says, pulling himself off the bed, ignoring the tissues I've handed him and wiping his snotty nose on his sleeve. 'I reckon it was Miss Scarlett in the billiard room with the revolver, anyway.'

'Bollocks,' I say. 'She did it in the ballroom. With the spanner.'

chapter eleven

Funny, isn't it, how stuff doesn't always seem to go to plan? Somehow in my own mind, I had that Sunday all worked out. We were going to see Mum in the morning. Have a chat, talk about Jesse's football triumph. Then head home for lunch with Mrs M. Sunday was always a roast with Mrs M, we were relieved to discover, because there's only so much anyone can do to mess up a roast chicken. She'd had a good stab at it the previous week though by getting her gravy granules and the instant coffee mixed up (her eyesight obviously isn't what it used to be), but fortunately I'd sniffed out the error before she'd managed to get it to the table, never mind actually slooshing the dirty brown coffee-flavoured goo over the meat and veg.

Mrs M always goes to church first thing on a Sunday morning, and, despite the fact she always drops massive hints about us joining her (she tells us what horrible little pagans we are), somehow we always manage to wheedle our way out. I plead excessive homework and Jesse gives her his big doe-eyed routine and that usually wins her over. So, as soon as she trots off down the path, safely out of the way, Jesse and I chuck on our clothes and hot-foot it over to the hospital on our bikes.

Visiting hours are always a bit strict during the week, but at weekends they seem to relax a lot more. But when we walk on to Nelson Ward this morning I can tell something is up. As we approach Mum's bed, Jesse and I start to slow down until eventually we stop about three metres away. The bed is empty, made up and ready for the next occupant.

Jesse and I look at each other.

'Where is she?' he asks.

I look blankly at the hospital bed.

All I can do is shrug.

The staff nurse, Jasmine, comes sailing towards us. We like her. Well, Mum likes her, which normally means that we like her too. Mum rates all the nurses on a purely professional basis. 'Sloppy,' she'd say about Kim, Luiz is 'kind and caring, a very good nurse', Heather is 'lazy and grunts a lot' and Ginny is declared 'a laugh'.

'Hello, boys, you're up with the lark this morning, aren't you?'

Jasmine is checking a chart with her usual air of efficiency.

'Where's Mum?' I ask, bluntly.

'Didn't someone phone you yesterday?' she says, scowling. 'Kim was meant to call you. Your mum's been moved to another ward. Spencer. It's on the fourth floor.'

'Spencer?'

Jesse's bottom lip has started to quiver a bit. I know it sounds kind of wet, but I can't help feeling sorry for him. All he wants to do is tell Mum about his football match, have her rub his back and tell him what a star he is. It just seems like he's got to perform the trials of Hercules first.

'Tell you what,' says Jasmine, noticing Jesse's lip and taking him by the hand, 'why don't I get Luiz to take you boys up in the lift?'

We stand in the lift with Luiz, chatting away. He's a tall Brazilian bloke, always has a smile for us, always stops to chat when we visit. He loves teasing Jesse about football too.

'Your England lose again I see,' he smiles. His English isn't fantastic, but it's a lot better than our Portuguese. 'Still, what you expect? Your English players spend too much time worrying about their hair and not enough time practising, I think.'

'Brazilian players don't have any hair,' says Jesse. 'They're all bald as coots.'

Luiz rubs his own close-cropped balding head.

'What, like me, you think?' He laughs. 'I save a fortune on the hair cuts and shampoo, you know.'

The lift pings at the fourth floor, the doors sweep open and we all pile out. Jesse has relaxed a bit, chatting to Luiz, and we walk towards the swing doors.

'Why've they moved Mum up here?' I ask.

'It's a special ward,' says Luiz. 'She's better here, I think. They understand more about her illness on Spencer. She has her own room too. Wait here while I go and see the desk, please.'

I'm thinking, illness? What illness? I thought they were still doing tests.

Luiz approaches the nurse at the desk and explains something in a low voice. She turns to look at us as he speaks, then she bites her lip and nods. Luiz returns with her.

'This is Megan,' says Luiz. 'I leave you with her now, yes?' He ruffles Jesse's hair. 'Spend more time practising and less time doing your hair, Jesse, and you may play for England one day, eh?'

'If I go bald I can always play for Brazil,' Jesse says.

Luiz is laughing as he dives back into the lift.

'Your mum's in here,' says Megan, and she leads us into a side room off the main ward.

83

Mum is lying propped up in the bed with some kind of monitor attached to her arm. She looks really dopey, but she opens her eyes and just says, 'Boys . . .' and holds her arms out to us.

Jesse launches himself into them and Megan says, 'Hey there, easy, Tiger, your mum's not a well woman, you know. I'll just get you a couple of chairs.'

'Oh, I've missed you both,' says Mum. She raises her arm – the one with the funny little contraption attached – and traces the side of my face with her fingers, very gently. She smiles at me. I notice her face is much thinner, and her hair looks lank and greasy. The sun is flooding through her window – it's another lovely day – but Mum just looks grey and tired, really knackered.

'What's this for?' I ask, pointing at the little box with the digital display.

'Is it a kind of iPod?' says Jesse, gormlessly. Duh.

'It's for pain relief,' says Mum. 'See, when the pain gets bad, I can just press on this little red button here, and it gives me something to make it better.'

Megan slips two chairs into the room, and closes the door behind her. I sit down on one, but Jesse just lies across Mum's bed.

'What does it give you?' Jesse asks.

'It's a drug,' says Mum.

'Drugs!' said Jesse. 'You're always going on at us

about the dangers of drugs . . .'

'Not those kinds of drugs, lard brain,' I say.

'It's medicine,' says Mum patiently. 'It's to help take the pain away, help me feel better. Luke darling, can you pass me some water please? I'm so thirsty at the moment.'

I pour Mum out a glass of water and give it to her. I watch her hand take hold of the glass and notice how thin her wrists are, how the skin is practically translucent, almost as fragile as the glass she's holding.

Jesse starts telling Mum all about his finest hour on the pitch.

She smiles and laughs as he exaggerates his role out of all proportion. I'm thinking she looks better already.

When he's finished, she looks up at me.

'So how's my big grown-up boy?' she says.

'Okay,' I say.

'I haven't had any breakfast yet,' says Jesse. 'Have you got anything to eat, Mum?'

Mum scowls.

'Isn't she feeding you, Mrs McLafferty?'

I give Jesse a subtle dig in the ribs. 'Yeah, yeah,' I tell her. 'We were just in a bit of a rush to get here. Jesse wanted to tell you all about the match. Did you eat breakfast?'

'Not really,' she says. 'I haven't much of an appetite these days.'

She points towards a sad, pappy-looking apple and a

spotty banana that's seen better days.

'There's some fruit . . .'

'Can I get something from the shop?' asks Jesse. 'Please? I'm starving.'

I can tell Mum is quite keen to get rid of Jesse, because normally she'd bang on about not buying loads of sweets and fizzy drinks and rubbish like that. Only this time, she doesn't, she just gives him the money and doesn't remind him to bring back the change like she normally does. He's out of the door in a micro-second.

'I want to talk to you, Luke,' says Mum.

She holds out her hand, so pale it could be porcelain, and takes mine in it. I thought it would feel cold, but it's not, it's warm, slightly clammy.

'They've been waiting to move me up to Spencer because . . .' she pauses for breath as she struggles to choose the right words, ' . . . because now they know what's wrong with me, they can give me specialist treatment here.'

'I know,' I say. 'That's what Luiz told us.'

'They're starting me on other treatments now too,' says Mum. 'Some of them leave me feeling tired and washed-out. I spend all my time wishing I was at home with you two, worrying about how you're getting on without me, but then sometimes I'm quite glad you can't see me in this state.'

'When are you coming home, Mum?' I ask.

She glances up at me and her eyes look glassy and bright, and then everything starts spilling over, there are tears running down her cheeks and I notice she's squeezing my hand really hard.

'I'm coming home for the weekend in a couple of weeks' time,' says Mum. 'I've had a word with the staff here, and they can make special arrangements. They'll drop me off on the Friday night and send a special nurse. Mia is going to come too. Then they'll pick me up and drop me back on the Sunday.'

'Just for the weekend?' I say. I don't understand. All we've talked about over the last few weeks is Mum getting better, Mum coming home, what we'll do when Mum gets back. Now she's coming home and she's going back again. And she's not even better. That's not right.

'Just for the weekend,' says Mum, and she starts to cry again. I've only ever seen her cry once before all this and that was after Dad left. I came down one night, about half an hour after I'd gone to bed, and I found her crying on the sofa. She looked really embarrassed, like I'd caught her out, and tried to wipe her face with the back of her sleeve, but I could tell she'd been crying.

'I'm not really well enough to come home for good, not yet,' she says.

She gulps. She wants to say something, but the words aren't coming out. She's stuck.

'You've got cancer, haven't you?' I say.

Mum raises a hand to her eyes as though she's trying to protect them from the sun. It looks as if she's trying to cover the tears, cover the pain, she can't bear to look at me. She turns her head to the side, but she can't speak, as though something has lodged in her throat – maybe it's the words, maybe it's the cancer – and then she starts to cry again, really sobbing this time. She holds her arms out to take me, like she used to do when I was little, and she'd pick me up and twirl me around in the garden and my head would spin. That's my cue to go to her, to hold her and hug her back, but she feels like bones and paper, she's lost so much weight and I don't want to hurt her. I can feel her sobbing in my arms in big, shuddering spasms, as though everything is broken and it'll never be mended again.

'I wanted to tell you,' she gasps. 'But I couldn't say it. I just couldn't say that word.'

chapter twelve

'I'll not be here that weekend,' announces Mrs M over lunch. 'I'm going to visit my sister Margaret in Colchester. She's a cleaner at a local school there and she's a martyr to her bunions.'

She sniffs and takes another sip of her pale ale. It's her tipple of choice at Sunday lunchtime. I'd never even heard of it before she came to live with us. We're allowed juice that Mrs M always calls 'squash'.

Mrs M isn't happy with us. Of course, she got back from church before we did and once she realised where we'd bunked off to – Jesse's rubbish at keeping secrets, he blurted it out as soon as we got back – she threw a wobbly.

'The hospital specifically asked me to keep you away this weekend,' she said. 'That nurse told me your mother's not well enough for visitors. And there you go, sneaking off up there to pester the poor woman as soon as I'm off to church. You'll drive that woman to an early grave.'

She's still seething as we pick our way through a semi-incinerated roast chicken, so the conversation isn't exactly flowing. I'm chewing on some semi-raw broccoli and Jesse is cutting the burnt bits off a carrot when he looks up at her.

'It'll be good having Mum at home again,' he says brightly. 'Even if it is just for the weekend.'

'That'll be nice for the two of yous,' says Mrs M. She gets up from the table and carries her plate to the sink. I've noticed she always has half as much as Jesse and me at mealtimes, pecking away like a demented bird some days, but mostly she hardly touches it. I've a sneaking suspicion she's getting decent food smuggled in during the night.

'I'm making myself scarce so you boys can spend some time alone with your mammy . . . while you can.' Her voice trails off as she says the last bit, as though she's saying something she shouldn't be. I think about the cancer again.

I hadn't said anything to Jesse on the way back from the hospital. Mum said to keep it as 'our secret' because she didn't want Jesse getting upset. It felt as though we were parents conspiring together not to tell the children. It made me realise that Mum doesn't think of me as a kid any more.

We'd spent the rest of the visit discussing what we would do when she came home. We'll have to bring Jesse's bed down for Mum from upstairs, and Mum said Jesse could sleep in her bed for the weekend, which of course isn't just Mum's bed anymore but Mrs McLafferty's too. Mum said she'll ask Mrs M to change the bedding before she goes (she could see the horrified look on Jesse's face at the idea of sleeping on Mrs M's sheets) and then we discussed watching DVDs, what food we'd eat and what games we'd play, as though we were planning Christmas.

It's only now that I realise how much our lives have changed lately. Normally we'd have a takeaway on a Friday night, a curry or a Chinese, or get out a DVD from the corner shop. Jesse would snuggle up to Mum on the sofa and I'd lounge over a chair and stick my feet up on the coffee table. I'd get told off for doing that during the week, but somehow on a Friday night I'd get away with it.

Friday night was our night, a time to chill out and wind down after the hassles of the week. I know it's going to be different this particular Friday. I know Mum's bed is going to be in the lounge, and we'll have to help her. But who cares? At least Mum will be at home. At least we'll be together.

Mrs McLafferty bangs down two bowls in front of Jesse and me.

'Rhubarb crumble and custard,' she announces unnecessarily. It's what she serves every Sunday. The health-giving properties of rhubarb are one of Mrs M's favourite topics of conversation, but I notice she isn't eating any herself. She's standing by the window, looking out into the garden and smoking. The custard has been sitting on the crumble for a few minutes now and there's a shrunken skin formed on the top.

'D'you want your skin?' Jesse says, though he's already wedged his spoon underneath the plasticky yellow layer and is greedily transferring it from my bowl to his.

'That grass needs cutting before your mother comes home,' says Mrs M. 'There's a little job for you, Luke.'

'We need to make a banner,' says Jesse. 'A proper welcome home banner. You know, with *WELCOME HOME, MUM* in big letters, that we can hang across the front door. She'll like that.'

This smacks a little of reception class to me, but I don't want to curb Jesse's unbridled enthusiasm. I still keep hearing the word 'cancer' ringing round my head, and I'm thinking I've just got to play along with him. But once he starts cutting up magazines to make each letter a different colour, I get caught up in his excitement and start joining in.

Mrs M says, 'Make sure you don't get any of that glue stuff on my table. It's a swine to get off.'

'It's not her table,' I whisper to Jesse under my breath. 'It's ours.'

'Oh yes,' says Jesse, as though he's only just realised it's our house she's living in and not the other way round.

He turns round quickly to check she's not looking and then squirts a blob of glue under the newspaper that she's made us lay over the entire table.

'That'll teach her.'

'I'm just going to take the weight off my feet,' says Mrs M and waddles out to the lounge. It's time for her 'Sunday afternoon constitutional', as she calls it, which means she's going to snooze her way through the omnibus edition of *EastEnders*. I reckon now's a good time to hatch a plan.

'Listen, that weekend we get her out.'

Jesse's cutting orange bits up for the 'U' of *MUM*.

'She's going anyway,' he says.

'No, I mean get her out for good,' I say. 'Mia's the one who found Mrs M and she's coming to see Mum on Friday. So that's our chance to show Mia what an old nightmare she's dumped on us.'

'How are we going to do that?' says Jesse, poking his tongue out between his lips as he concentrates on the smooth lines of the U.

'We trash the upstairs so Mum can't tell,' I say. 'We don't want her getting involved, she'll only get upset.

Then we let Mia go upstairs and she can see for herself. We let her draw her own conclusions. Trust me, it's better that way.'

'Oh I get it,' says Jesse, looking up from his U which is definitely looking a bit lopsided. 'Mum's stuck downstairs in the lounge so she can't get upstairs to see the mess.'

'Eureka. See, you're not as stupid as you look.' I start cutting out the second M for *MUM*. I'm actually quite enjoying this but I'm not letting on.

'Okay,' says Jesse, and a big smile spreads across his face. 'So, when do we start trashing?'

chapter thirteen

'Twice round the perimeter should warm you up,' Freya explains. 'Then we'll do a few stretching exercises.'

It's Monday afternoon and Jesse's second training session with Joan of Arc's answer to Karren Brady.

Jesse nods at Freya – he doesn't moan or complain – then he starts jogging off up the track. The rec (short for recreation ground) is less of a park and more of a wasteland really, and probably one of the least attractive wastelands you're ever likely to see. There aren't that many people around, but maybe that's why she chose it. There's some dodgy-looking kid smoking a spliff and walking a Staffordshire bull terrier that looks like it's been reared on blood and guts rather than Pedigree Chum, and there are a couple of boys messing around on their skateboards. A middle-aged woman with dyed red hair is jogging unbelievably slowly. It's like watching the London Eye. Unless you look closely, you can't quite tell that she's moving at all.

'I don't know why you're still trying to make Jesse believe you can actually help him,' I tell Freya as Jesse jogs out of earshot. 'You don't know the first thing about football training.'

Freya stands with a hand on her hip.

'He's actually improved a lot in the past week,' says Freya. 'Anyway, what's eating you? What are you so sore about?'

'You're a charlatan,' I tell her. 'A big fake. You can't train Jesse properly and you know it. If that other kid, Darren Whatsisname, is better, he'll get a place on the team and there's nothing you can do to stop him. You're just setting Jesse up for a big fall.'

'In your opinion,' says Freya. 'Why do you think I've never mentioned my interest in football to you?'

I shrug. 'Because you're not that interested.'

'Wrong,' she says matter-of-factly. 'I am that interested. But you're not. You automatically assume that because it's of no interest to you, it's of no interest to anyone else. I know you well enough, Luke, to know that I'd be wasting my time talking about football with you. I can talk to you about movies and music and all kinds of stuff. But football? Forget it. What would be the point? Anyway, if I want to talk footie tactics, I can do that with David.' David's her dad. She stops for breath and then continues, 'Oh and "that other kid" as you call him is Duane Mulholland. And I can make sure Jesse has an edge over him. Just watch.'

'David?' This is all news to me. 'What's he got to do with anything?'

'When we lived in Southampton he used to coach my brother's team. I learned a lot from turning up to training sessions with him.'

That's Freya. Always full of surprises.

The rest of the week drags of course, because when you're desperately looking forward to something it takes ages to happen. Mrs M has a little phrase for it. She says 'a watched kettle never boils', and for once I think she may not be talking out of her wrinkly old tights. If I had a calendar, I suppose I'd be crossing the days off with a big black marker pen. Mum's looking forward to it too, I know.

I go to see her on Wednesday while Jesse has his next training session with Freya. Mum's having a visit from Polly, her Macmillan nurse. I'd never heard of Macmillan nurses before, but Mum explained that they help people like her through their illness (she didn't say the 'c' word but I knew that's what she meant). It can be anything from practical help to just someone to talk to when you're feeling down, or worried, or lonely. Mum says Polly's been great at organising her weekend at home.

Mum's told me a lot about Polly. She is quite young

and slightly kookie. She rides round on a bicycle that looks like it's a Victorian original, with a basket at the front. She buys all her clothes from charity shops and her life is like some kind of soap opera. She's going out with this bloke called Colin, who's a plumber, and she moans about him all the time. Mum says Polly's only going out with Colin because she fancies his mate, Gray, who's an insurance salesman (again, not the most interesting career choice), but in the evenings and at weekends, Gray plays guitar in a rock band called Hub and Polly reckons they're going to be BIG. Her eyes open wide when she says the word 'big' and I think she's got it bad for Gray. Polly spends a lot of time sitting and chatting with Mum about things that don't involve pain relief and chemotherapy and all those other words that have slipped into our vocabulary while we weren't looking.

Anyway, when I arrive, Polly is sitting in a full-length floaty floral number at the end of Mum's bed, a big straw hat by her side, yacking away at full pelt. She's got this really pretty face with long-ish brown hair and she waves her hands about as she talks as though she's conducting an orchestra. She and Mum are laughing.

'Heard lots about you,' Polly says as Mum introduces us.

I never know what to say when people say that.

Adults normally say something like 'all good, I hope,' or crack some other corny joke, but I just nod and smile and Polly says, 'Is that nutcase brother of yours behaving himself?' like she knows Jesse really well, and I say, 'I don't know, he's all wrapped up in footie practice at the moment,' and she says, 'God, he sounds like my boyfriend, Colin. What is it about blokes and football? Is there some kind of unwritten rule that says men can only talk about football?'

Then Mum says, 'Luke's not a big football fan, are you, love?' and I say, 'No, not really,' and Polly says, 'Oh, there is hope for us all then. Hurry up and grow up, Luke, so I can marry you,' and she starts laughing and Mum joins in too. Although I hardly know her, I can tell I like her already.

Everything is set for the weekend. Polly is coming home with Mum on Friday night to make sure she's all settled in and we know what to do in case of any emergencies. Nobody really elaborates on what an emergency might be, but that's probably just as well. I know Mum's pain gets really bad sometimes. It's mainly her back and shoulder that hurt and occasionally even the painkillers don't seem to touch it. On Sunday, while I was talking to her, she suddenly started breathing really deeply and pressing her painkiller machine like mad and I could tell it was bad because she just seemed to disappear off into another place, somewhere she really didn't want to be, somewhere that hurt like hell. She held on to my hand and squeezed it really hard, and I pressed the button to get the nurse, and the nurse told her to 'ride through it', as though Mum was surfing or swooping down a rollercoaster ride or doing something quite pleasant, and not suffering some horrible, twisting, gouging pain that forced her breath out in big gasping shudders.

Polly bounces off the bed and gathers up the basket for her bike, declaring she'll 'zip off home, now', but we can call her on her mobile at any time, even the middle of the night.

'Any excuse to get away from Colin,' says Polly, winking, and Mum says, 'You're terrible, you are,' and Polly replies, 'And that's why you like me!' and gives Mum a kiss and plants another on my cheek before I can look embarrassed. Then she flounces out, singing, 'See you at the weekend!', grappling with the straw hat and the bike lock that she produces from the basket.

'I got a call from your Uncle Stu last night,' says Mum. 'He didn't sound his usual perky self. Still, I suppose that's the joy of being unemployed.'

Since Mum's been in hospital, Uncle Stu's been on the phone to her every couple of days. He keeps threatening to come and visit since he hasn't found a new job yet. Seems there aren't that many jobs for translators in Manchester right now.

'Not having a lot of luck as a family, are we?' sighs Mum. 'Me laid up like this, Stu on the dole.'

She pushes her hair back off her face and I can see a couple of strands come away in her hand. She pulls them out and holds them up to the light as though it's something precious, hair that she can spin into gold, like some fairytale princess.

'Look at this,' she says, as though she's only just noticed she's losing her hair. We haven't mentioned it up until now – it's not a great conversation opener with your mum when she's fighting cancer, 'Oh, I see you're looking a bit balder today, Mum' – but it's definitely been getting thinner, which must mean it's falling out. So I've just kept quiet about it, thinking maybe she hadn't noticed. Of course she's noticed. Who wouldn't?

'It's starting to fall out. They said it might.' She rubs it absent-mindedly into a little hairball in her hands. 'I'll need a wig at this rate.'

She looks at me. I don't know what to say, I haven't a clue what to do. Mum forces her mouth into a smile, and bends her face closer to mine.

'Mind you, I've always quite fancied a wig,' she says. 'What do you reckon, Dolly Parton or Cher?' And she smiles and softly kisses me on my cheek.

chapter fourteen

I must admit, I did think about bunking off school on Friday to try and get the house ready for Mum, but then I remembered that we are meant to be trashing the upstairs later so there didn't seem much point. Anyway, Friday is double art and I'm doing this pottery self-portrait which I'm really getting into. It's a head-and-shoulders three-dimensional clay version of me, and I've just got to the stage where I'm going to apply the glaze. I'm not so great at this sort of thing but my model seems to have taken on a life of its own. Even Mr Magni, our pottery teacher, reckons it's a good likeness.

'I'd recognise your ugly mug anywhere,' he said to me when I showed it to him. He's all right, is Mr Magni. He walks around listening to an iPod and singing along off-key. They should be firing our self-portraits in the kiln next week, and I'm going to give mine to Mum to keep next to her bed. At the moment she's only got this terrible old photo. I must be nine and I'm wearing what looks like a grey balaclava, and Jesse's about seven and clutching his favourite soft toy at the time, a rabbit called Englebert. Everyone picks it up and says, 'Ah, sweet', which is a little irritating when you're fourteen and would quite like to burn every balaclava in the world to wreak revenge.

Straight after school, Jesse and I rush to get back home before Mum and Polly. We're working on a tight schedule here. Mum's due in at about five-thirty, so we're going to have to shift it some to get the upstairs looking pretty rank. As soon as I open the front door, we know what we're up against. Jesse and I are nearly overcome by the overwhelming fumes of lavender furniture polish that come wafting out. It's Mrs M's trademark scent. She thinks the smell of the stuff is the sign of a clean home. I've even seen her squirting it around like air freshener. It wouldn't surprise me if she spritzed it behind her ears too.

'Phwooarh, it stinks in here,' says Jesse, gasping for breath as he closes the door behind us. 'Pass me a gas mask, please.'

Mrs M was heading off to her sister at lunchtime, she said, but she must have been round the house like a demon, dusting and hoovering for all she was worth before she headed off to the darkest depths of Colchester. The cushions are looking nicely plumped, every surface gleams, and the vase on the mantelpiece is buffed up like a diamond.

We head upstairs to check the state of the bedrooms. To be honest, ours aren't exactly pristine, but they're not that bad either. Mrs M obviously realised that Mum wasn't going to be running a testing finger over the surfaces up here, so she's concentrated her cleaning blitz downstairs. Very sneaky. True to her word, Mrs M's also changed the bedlinen on Mum's bed for Jesse.

'At least I won't have to sleep in her smelly sheets,' he says. 'I bet her farts stink of rhubarb crumble.'

'Come on, get a move on,' I tell him. 'We've only got about an hour before Mum and Mia get back. We need to get trashing.'

We head upstairs. Now for someone who has a natural talent for making a mess (and it's true, I'm not so bad at it myself), Jesse proves to be pretty lousy at deliberately fouling up the upstairs of 47 Colbourne Way. I tell him to start in Mum/Mrs M's bedroom, and he half-heartedly throws the pillows on the floor and knocks a chair over. Then he sits down on the bed.

'This isn't as easy as it sounds,' he moans.

'Don't be such a wimp,' I tell him. 'Look, do you want to get rid of Mrs M or not? I'm not doing this just for me, you know. Stomp this into the rug.'

I tip the contents of a full ashtray that lies by the side of the bed on to the shaggy rug. Then I fling open

Mum's wardrobe and start chucking the contents around.

'I know,' says Jesse, finally cottoning on as he grinds the ash and butts into the pile with his heel. 'The rubbish bin.'

He picks up a bin from the corner of the room and starts strewing the contents about. It's got empty fag packets, loads of sweet wrappers (seems Mrs M loves her Rolos) and what looks like a big clump of hair that she must have scraped off a hairbrush – disgusting. There's also a used tin of talc that I shake about a bit, although, urgh, it stinks of her, and then Jesse finds all this paper rammed down into the bottom of the basket.

'What's all that?' I ask. Jesse is chucking it up in the air, like some cheesy Euro Jackpot billionaire. He's definitely getting the hang of this now.

'I dunno.' He stops a minute. 'It's rubbish, isn't it?'

I'm delving back into the bin and extract a handful of envelopes, unopened envelopes. Big bloody hell. There's a whole load of stuff. Bills, get well cards, mailouts from school, the child benefit people, loads of official stuff. All addressed to Mum. All unceremoniously dumped without being opened. I can't believe it.

Jesse stops scattering and looks over my shoulder.

'Where d'you find that?'

'At the bottom of the bin,' I tell him. 'You didn't put

this stuff in here, did you?'

He looks at me in amazement. 'Shut up. What would I do a thing like that for?'

'What would she want to do a thing like that for?' I say. 'This is Mum's mail. Her private property. It's nothing to do with Mrs McLafferty.'

'Why is she chucking it away?' asks Jesse. 'I don't get it.'

'I'm not sure,' I say. 'It's like she's pretending Mum doesn't exist any more. She's been slowly taking over her home and her life. And it's stealing. We could report her to the police for this . . .'

'Bloody old cow.'

Jesse's nostrils are flaring in a dangerous way. I know that look. It's a sure sign he's about to lose it. Next thing I know, he's flying down the stairs, screaming, and heads for the kitchen. When I get in there, he's strewing Rice Krispies all over the kitchen worktop like a thing possessed.

'I'll show her,' he snarls. 'She's our mum. She can't just shove her in the bin. Let's mess up her kitchen.' And with that, he tips the kitchen bin on its side and kicks it, leaving a trail of stinky smelly garbage across the floor. As he does it, I can see a wild, demonic look in his eye, and I think, yeah, he's right. Let's mess up Mrs M where it hurts most. Right here in the kitchen. Let's show her.

'Hold up,' I say. 'What we need is a little music. Something we can trash to properly.'

I run upstairs and quickly rummage through my CD collection.

'Gotcha!'

I jump back downstairs, two steps at a time.

'Just the thing.'

I whack on the old kitchen CD player and give the volume a bit of welly. 'Teenage Dirtbag' comes bellowing out.

Jesse starts whooping like a loony and chucking stuff all round the kitchen. Instant coffee, rice, bread. I'm crumbling up the remains of a packet of digestives over his head, jumping around and screaming to the music. Jesse opens the fridge and grabs a yogurt and lobs it at me, overhand, like he's chucking a grenade into a trench. I watch it rise and, I have to say, he's timed it to perfection. There's a beautiful arc as the yogurt flies through the air and, like some evil buzz bomb, it just stops and starts to plummet. As it drops, it picks up speed. It's all happening in slow motion but, as I watch, I suddenly realise it's heading straight for me. I try to dodge, but it's all too late, and the little plastic pot whacks me on the side of the head then bounces off and smashes against the window. There's a big smear of strawberry yogurt running down the pane of glass now, and I've got a yogurt scar streaked across my forehead. Jesse bursts out laughing as though this is the funniest thing he's ever seen. He's laughing so hard he can hardly get his sentence out which comes in short, hysterical gasps.

'You . . . look like . . . Harry Potter!'

I grab the nearest thing to hand: a jar of Olde English chunky-cut marmalade that Mrs M slathers all over her toast every morning after she's had her first fag of the day. I twist open the lid and scoop out a pile of the sweet, sticky, orangey mess on my hand. Jesse tries to bolt for the door, shrieking with laughter still, but I've put the jar down now and I'm grabbing him with my other hand and smearing marmalade across his face. Then I reach out for the porridge, and tip the box all over his head. He looks like he's got some hideous skin condition, standing there, still convulsed with laughter, his face covered with nasty bubbled contusions, and porridge oats dropping into his open mouth.

I'm laughing too, and now he's chucking cornflakes at me like a demon. We can both tell that this trashing business is getting out of hand, but it's too late now. Something within has just snapped, something tight and taut and pent-up, and it just feels so good. We give in to it, abandoning ourselves completely in a morass of mess. It's as though we're participating in some weird kind of pagan ritual, throwing things at each other, tipping anything we can lay our hands on over our heads. There are herbs and honey and sugar and cereals and jam flying across the kitchen. You name it, we're chucking it around like a pair of naughty chimps, howling uproariously with laughter. Jesse is laughing so much that he's clutching at his groin, which normally means he's in danger of actually wetting himself. As a kid he used to do this quite often, and Mum would always try and blame me, presumably to make Jesse feel less embarrassed.

'Don't make him laugh like that,' she'd say. 'You know he can't control himself,' when she actually meant, 'You know he can't control his bladder'. Meanwhile Jesse would scamper off to the loo clutching his nether regions with a big dark stain the shape of Africa emerging on his shorts.

I can see he's reaching the point of no return now, when he chucks a mushed-up-looking banana that's already been back and forth a couple of times and yanks the door open to rush off to the loo.

And there he is. A bloke, just standing there in the kitchen doorway with his mouth hanging open, a bag in one hand that he lets drop to the floor.

Jesse just lets out a wail and dashes off up the stairs; the lettuce I've armed myself with from the fridge falls to the floor with a swish and Uncle Stu says, 'Bloody hell fire, it looks like the lunatics have taken over the asylum.'

chapter fifteen

By the time Jesse has come back downstairs, all spruced up and wearing a *dry* pair of trousers, I notice, I'm on the receiving end of Uncle Stu's wrath, and believe me, he's in full flow. This is a side of Uncle Stu I have not previously seen. He's chucking about some rather grown-up words in the same kind of way that Jesse and I were both hurling breakfast cereals around the kitchen just a few minutes previously.

'Your mother is due home for the first time in several . . . several weeks,' he says. He's speaking quite slowly because he's:

   a) making a point

   and

   b) absolutely furious.

'Do you two know how ill your mother is?' he demands.

'Yes,' I say. 'I do. She's very ill.'

I'm keeping all answers to a minimum and speaking very quietly. I find that works best when adults don't really want you to contribute, but they do want you to grovel profusely.

'Then what the hell are you playing at?' he roars. 'What kind of welcome do you call this?' He's pacing backwards and forwards now, like some kind of demented sergeant major giving his troops a proper rollicking.

'She could be home any minute now, and she's going to walk into this . . . this . . .'

I can tell he's trying to find some word to sum it all up without swearing, but he can't quite pull it off.

' . . . this shit heap.'

Jesse has such a serious look on his face that I can tell he's in danger of bursting out laughing. I know that look. If he starts laughing now, it'll be disastrous. We're both in the poo as it is.

'Really sorry, Uncle Stu,' I mutter, hanging my head in shame. A drip of jam falls off the end of my nose, on to the tiled floor. 'I don't know what came over us.'

'Right, well, I don't know how long you've got . . .' he looks at his watch, 'but you'd better get cleaning – this place and yourselves. I'll make a start upstairs and you two can sort out the kitchen.'

'Yes, Uncle Stu,' we murmur together, like a couple of pre-school kids caught misbehaving.

'And get a move on,' he says. 'We haven't got all day.'

Today is turning into some freak game show, and I have to admit it's all of our own making. First you trash the place, then you clean it up, and you're racing against the clock. Oh, and by the way, there's no car to be won.

Uncle Stu snaps the Wheatus CD off, and although I could really do with a bit of music to jolly things along, this is probably not the best time to put in a request. Instead I take off upstairs in search of clean clothes and a quick shower.

'What's he doing here anyway?' says Jesse when I come back down, sweeping a pile of dry macaroni and lentils up. 'It was meant to be just Mum and us this weekend, wasn't it? I don't remember anyone inviting him.'

'Maybe nobody told him,' I say.

I've got to admit, I'm feeling kind of silly. I mean, I've hardly seen this guy in years and suddenly he's standing in front of us in his jeans and polo shirt like some Ralph Lauren ad while we behave like some kids straight out of the infants. It's not a great way to make an impression.

After about forty-five minutes, the kitchen is almost back to normal. There's still yogurt dripping down the window, but as Jesse threw that one, I figure it's his job to sort it. I just point at it and say 'Yours' and he seems to understand. He doesn't even bother to argue, which is something of a first for Jesse.

I can still hear cleaning noises coming from upstairs. I decide to raise my head above the parapet and head up to Mum's bedroom.

'How's it going?' I say as I walk in gingerly.

'Yeah, nearly done.' He has his back to me, but I can tell from the tone of his voice that most of the anger has abated. 'We need to bring Jesse's bed down for your mum,' says Uncle Stu. 'Perhaps you can give me a hand to help carry it, Luke?' He pauses for a moment. 'Unless you're thinking about chucking it down the stairs?'

'I'm sorry,' I tell him as we go into Jesse's room. 'We both went a bit mental there. I really don't know what happened.'

'Not like you,' says Uncle Stu, 'You're not usually tearaways – not according to your mum anyway. Maybe that Mrs McLafferty has been getting you into bad habits . . .'

'Oh her,' I say. 'Let's not go there.' I'll tell him about her secret life as a letter-snatcher later. It could tip him over the edge right now.

Jesse saunters in. Always quick to pick up on a change of mood, he tries to keep off the subject of mess and furniture.

'Uncle Stu,' says Jesse, plonking himself down on the bed we're about to move, 'what are you doing here anyway? You never told us you were coming.'

'I spoke to your mum on the phone yesterday and she told me she was home for the weekend. Said she was worried about how she was going to cope with it all, though.'

'We'll be all right,' I say. 'Polly's bringing her back and she says she'll pop in tomorrow too. And Mia's coming round.'

'Well, I've had a quiet week,' says Uncle Stu. 'I had an interview on Tuesday and nothing since. So I thought I'd give your mum a bit of a surprise. Drove down at lunchtime to spring a little visit on her.'

'And you're the one who ended up surprised,' says Jesse, trying to make light of the situation. Uncle Stu's not ready to laugh it off yet, I can tell.

'How did you get in, anyway?' I ask.

'You two bloody nanas left the key in the door.' He tuts out loud and shakes his head. For once, it actually feels really good to have an adult in the house. Well, one who's not over sixty-five. Then the doorbell rings.

'Mum!' yells Jesse and goes stamping down the stairs. Suddenly he stops short.

'Wait! I haven't put my banner up yet . . .'

In all the confusion, Jesse's forgotten his beloved banner that he's spent the last two weeks on (with a little help from me). He races upstairs and brings it down. One end is handed to me, and he takes the other and stands nearer the door. It's a tight squeeze but you can make out the message, *WELCOME HOME, MUM.*

'Okay, Uncle Stu,' commands Jesse. 'Open the door.'

And there's Mum in a wheelchair with Polly standing behind shouting, 'Ta-da!' Mia is hovering in the background with some bags, and the paramedic who's driven Mum home is hanging about at the back of the ambulance. I'm relieved to notice that it isn't Sam who I threw up over a few weeks ago.

'Mum!' shouts Jesse and chucks himself at her as though he hasn't seen her for years.

'Jesse,' she murmurs and, although he's hugging her much too tightly, I can see her pale blue eyes sparkle and she's blinking back tears, and she's glad to be home. Her right hand cradles his head in the way that mothers hold their newborn babies. She doesn't want him to catch her crying though, so she's wiping the corners of her eyes furiously as though she promised herself this wouldn't happen, she wouldn't cry, and he wouldn't see. He doesn't notice. Everyone else seems to be sniffing a bit and turning their heads away and then Mum looks across and sees Uncle Stu and says 'Stuart . . .' in a strange, dreamy voice, as though she's questioning why he's here. It's almost as though she's in a trance, everything seems to be moving in slow-motion.

I'm a bit overwhelmed by the sight of Mum in a wheelchair. They're for disabled people or old people, aren't they? I never thought about how Mum was actually going to get home. Although she's always in bed when I see her, I suppose I thought she could still walk.

Polly moves towards me and hooks her arm through mine. 'Let's get the kettle on shall we, Luke? I'm desperate for one of my herbals . . .'

She propels me towards the kitchen, leaving the reception committee on the doorstep.

'Ooh, everything ship-shape and Bristol fashion in here.' She's as cheerful as ever, searching for teabags and pouring milk. 'Never go anywhere without these.' She waves a camomile teabag at me that she's produced from her basket.

'Mrs McLafferty looking after you all right, is she?' she enquires, eyes wide open, and I just nod and smile as I turn away to fill the kettle.

chapter sixteen

By the time we get the bed downstairs (the mattress isn't a problem, it's the base that proves to be a bit of a scrape-the-walls nightmare) and Mia's made it up for Mum, it's seven o'clock and time for another cup of tea. That's what seems to happen when you have sick people around you, I discover. You drink tea and eat biscuits.

'So what do you do, Uncle Stu?' says Polly. She leans forward with her chin on her hand.

'Do you mean what did I do, or what do I want to do next?' says Uncle Stu.

'Ah,' says Polly, 'that's what we actors call resting.'

'I thought you were a nurse,' I say.

'Oh, I am,' she says. 'But I've done a few jobs before. Actor, waitress, bartender, barista . . .' She ticks them off on her hand as she goes through her mental list. 'Multi-talented, me.'

'Barrister?' says Jesse. 'Do you have to wear a wig? In court?'

'Talking of which,' sighs Mum, and she runs her fingers through her hair again, and a few wisps hang from her fingers as if to prove the point. 'It's coming out in whacking great clumps now,' she exaggerates.

'Oh, Mia and I can sort you out tomorrow, no problem,' says Polly, as if buying wigs for balding women is the sort of thing she does every day. Well, maybe it is.

Mia nods and drains her mug. I get the impression she isn't comfortable talking about Mum's hair loss in front of 'the boys'.

'And I said "barista" not "barrister".' Polly leans forward towards Jesse and stage-whispers conspiratorially. 'It's a posh word they use in Starbucks for someone who makes the coffee.'

'You were a translator, weren't you, Stuart?' Mia asks. They've met a couple of times over the years, but not for ages.

'Yeah, German and Spanish,' says Uncle Stu. 'And a smattering of Cantonese. Though there doesn't seem to be much call for German these days. May have to retrain . . .'

'Mandarin and Cantonese,' says Polly knowingly. 'That's where the markets are moving. It's boom time in China.'

Mia is standing up, and she's holding Mum's hand.

'I need to get back to Andy and the kids,' she says, 'but you can call me any time, you know that. You've got all my numbers on your mobile haven't you, Patty?'

Mum nods.

'Don't keep her up too late tonight, she's looking worn out,' says Mia quietly to Uncle Stu as she passes him on her way out. 'I'll pop by tomorrow. Bye everyone.'

'Right,' says Uncle Stu, 'I don't know about you lot but I could eat a scabby horse festering with flies, and it's a bit late to start cooking, so what do you all say to a takeaway?'

'I really ought to be going too,' says Polly, standing up and reaching for her basket. 'But do you know there's an amazing little Italian pizza place up the road? Papa Giorgio's. I'll show you if you like.'

Once Polly and Uncle Stu have left, it's just me, Jesse and Mum, the way it always used to be. We have the telly blaring away in the background but to be honest, it's some rubbish talent show and we're not really watching.

'So what are we going to do tomorrow?' asks Jesse. 'You can come and see me play if you like. It's the semi-finals. We're playing Endymion Road at home.'

'She doesn't like,' I say. 'Mum's not up to seeing you and your footie-mad mates prancing around a field.'

'Yes, you are, aren't you, Mum?' says Jesse. 'You want to come and watch me play, don't you?'

'Course I do, love,' says Mum, trying to pull herself up a bit in the wheelchair. Although it's got her here (and I don't see how we would have done without it), it's a bit like a prison, confining her and hemming her in. I can see her pressing her finger on her pain-relief box, which means something is hurting bad.

'You okay, Mum?' I ask her.

She winces a little, as though, now I've noticed, she can stop pretending that she's feeling fine.

'Just my shoulder again,' she says. 'I think I may need one of those painkillers now, Luke, love.'

Polly has lined up all Mum's pills on the side in the kitchen and labelled them with what times we have to hand them out so we can't give her the wrong drugs. This is just as well as I don't fancy being had up for mumslaughter if I got them mixed up. She's also left some painkillers for times when Mum really needs them (like now). Mum knocks a couple back with the remains of her tea, and, although the TV is still spewing out its rubbish, she closes her eyes.

There's a ring on the door and Uncle Stu is back with the pizzas, some beer for him and there's ice cream and fizzy drinks too. Mum wouldn't normally allow this, (ice cream maybe, but not the drinks), but she doesn't say anything when he waves the stuff at us victoriously. We just grab a pile of plates and sit round in front of the telly getting stuck into the pizzas. Uncle Stu offers Mum a beer, but she says she's not sure if it goes well with heavy-duty painkillers ('I'm feeling a little woozy as it is') and she's not up to it anyway.

To be honest, it doesn't look like she's up to the pizza, either. While we set about the Al Capone (chilli beef with extra peppers) and Veggie Massacre (roast veg with extra mozzarella), Mum lies back and takes the odd nibble at a sad, solitary slice of pizza and a tiny bit of garlic bread.

'Not eating much, Pat?' Uncle Stu asks.

'It's the drugs,' says Mum. 'Don't have much of an appetite right now.'

'You'll need to keep your strength up, sis,' says Uncle Stu. 'Try and eat a bit more . . .'

She raises the pizza slice to her lips very slowly, and her hand has a slight shake to it, I notice.

'That's the girl,' he says, like she's a small child who just needs a little encouragement. But I notice she only takes the tiniest of bites, and the effort of raising the pizza to her mouth seems to have worn her out.

'What time is kick-off tomorrow then, Jesse?' asks Uncle Stu.

'Twelve noon,' says Jesse. 'Will you come too, Uncle Stu?'

'Course I will,' he says. 'Anyway, who's going to drive your mum to the match if I'm not there?'

chapter seventeen

Most Saturdays, the only thing that drags me out of bed is the prospect of a slice of hot buttered toast, a steaming great mug of tea and a lazy lounge on the sofa in front of some mid-morning kids' TV. But my body clock seems to have tuned in to Mum being back home again; when I check my alarm I find it's just gone eight and I'm wide awake.

Downstairs, I find I'm not the only one who's up with the lark. Uncle Stu is shovelling cornflakes down his throat (so we didn't scatter the whole box yesterday I'm relieved to discover) and Mia (where did she come from?) is sorting out Mum's medicine.

'I'll need a hand lifting Pat when she's finished,' she says to Uncle Stu.

I say my 'good mornings' and head towards the lounge to see Mum.

'Oh, give her a couple of minutes, love,' says Mia.

Then she drops her voice a tad and mouths, 'She's on the loo.'

'Oh,' I say. I don't like to point out that, before Mum got ill, Jesse and I were in and out of the bathroom constantly while Mum was on the loo, but somehow I suppose it's different when you have to be lowered on to a cold-looking bedpan and lifted off again when you've finished.

'According to the weather forecast,' says Uncle Stu, reading from the newspaper, 'it's wet and windy today but hot and sunny tomorrow. Now, hot and sunny Sunday says "barbecue" to me.'

He puts the paper down.

'What do you reckon, Luke? I don't suppose you lot have got such a thing as a barbecue out the back?'

'There should be one in the shed,' I say, ramming bread into the toaster. 'It may be a bit old and rusty, though. Don't think we used it at all last summer.'

In fact, I know we didn't. Because it rained all summer long, and even when it stopped raining, it looked like it was about to start again. Mum's never been a great barbecue fan, either. Although she's not exactly a bra-burning feminist, Mum believes blokes are just as capable as women of putting on the washing and clearing up the kitchen. And, although she's a dab hand with a screwdriver and she's redecorated the whole house at some stage, the art of the barbecue has somehow passed her by.

Uncle Stu is out the door like a whippet on steroids, diving into the shed and rummaging about with gusto. After a lot of clattering, he merges with a nasty blackened barbecue grill.

'It's all there,' he says. 'Good scrub and a bit of elbow grease and that'll do the job, I reckon. So what do you fancy? Sausages? Chicken? Burgers?'

Mia calls Unce Stu to go and help her with Mum, so I get handed the encrusted article and a Brillo pad that's going to transform this grease-fest into the best thing since a George Foreman grill. I haven't even had my toast yet.

'Give Golden Balls a shout, would you, Luke?' says Uncle Stu once Mia has gone. 'If he's going to be charging up and down the field in a couple of hours he'll need some breakfast inside him. Tell him I do a mean scrambled egg.'

'A barbecue?' says Jesse. 'We haven't had one for ages.'

We're driving to the footie match in Uncle Stu's car, and we're a bit late. Mum is sitting in the passenger seat, next to Uncle Stu. She's under a blanket although it's not that cold. Jesse is trying to put his kit on in the back of the car and he keeps kicking me, and kneeing me and shoving his elbow into my face as he struggles to get his footie shirt on. He keeps checking his bag every two minutes to make sure he hasn't forgotten his lucky troll.

'All the more reason to do it tomorrow,' she says. 'Not that I'm going to be much use, mind, in this thing . . .'

She tries to indicate her wheelchair but then realises she's not actually in it right now, and that seems to surprise her. It took a good fifteen minutes to get Mum in the car. Uncle Stu had to lift her in, fold down the wheelchair ('I've got a degree in languages, not engineering,' he muttered as he struggled with the release mechanism) and then try and squeeze it into the boot. Jesse, who could have been changing while this was going on, was looking on gormlessly, checking his watch every now and again as if that would help speed them up.

'Oh we don't need you,' says Uncle Stu, turning to Mum. 'I'm the barbecue king round here. And I've got my special helpers, right, guys?'

Once we're parked up, Jesse rushes off to join the team (he's put his shirt on inside out and hasn't even noticed, the dork), while Uncle Stu and I sort out the wheelchair and Mum. I seem to be better at getting the chair into position than Uncle Stu, so while I sort that, he lifts Mum out of the car.

'How much d'you weigh these days, Pat?' he asks.

Mum looks half asleep, but she smiles. 'Cheeky,' she

tells him. 'You should know never to ask a lady her weight.'

'We're going to have to fatten you up,' he says. 'You're all skin and bone, sis, like a little sparrow.'

He's holding Mum in his arms and gently lowering her into the chair. She raises her head slightly and plants a kiss on his cheek.

'There's a peck for you, then,' she says.

All this wheelchair malarkey has made something very obvious to me: Mum is actually quite frail and probably shouldn't be out here in the open air (especially when it looks like it might rain at any minute), watching a football match. Uncle Stu phoned Polly just before we left and asked her if she thought we ought to be taking Mum and she told him, 'It's her weekend, let her do whatever she wants. It'll probably do her a power of good.'

Mum said, 'I want to watch Jesse play,' and Uncle Stu said, 'You're meant to be taking it easy. Haven't you got some important knitting to do?' and Mum said, 'I'm your big sister and I may be ill, but I can still give you a very hard clip round the ear if you're not careful.'

Today, there's a fairly good crowd which I put down to the fact that it's the semi-finals. There's no sign of Jack or Freya though I reckon they may put in an appearance. But Uncle Stu makes up for them in the noise department. I swear, he's almost as loud as Jack's grandad's rattle. He shouts at all our players, bellows 'Come on now, Jesse!' every time the ball travels so much as ten metres within my brother's radar, and, when one of our Joan of Arc players gets booked for a dodgy tackle, he calls the ref a name that gets him a very stern look from Mum.

'It's all right,' he says by way of explanation. 'It's a football match. Swearing is all part of the fun.'

'There are children here, Stuart,' says Mum. 'So there's no need to call the poor bloke's parentage into question.'

'Are there?' Uncle Stu looks around as though he's observing the scene for the first time. 'D'you know, I hadn't even noticed . . .'

Perhaps it's Uncle Stu's very vocal support or perhaps it's Endymion Road's lack of any kind of defensive tactics. Whatever, the opposition certainly seems to be all over the place, and ten minutes before half-time, Ryan Dunbar boots a long ball up to Shav, who rips through the defence like a hot knife through butter and just taps the ball past the keeper. Easy.

The home crowd claps like mad – Uncle Stu manages to whistle really loud with his fingers stuck in his mouth – and even Mum manages to tap the side of her wheelchair and wave at Jesse, despite the fact that he had nothing to do with the goal.

At half-time when the oranges come out, Uncle Stu

gets a call from Polly on her mobile asking if Mum is still up for a bit of a shop later with Mia.

'Do you know,' says Mum, speaking her words slowly and deliberately, 'I think all this fresh air has worn me out? D'you think they could manage without me?'

Uncle Stu turns away and speaks quietly into the phone and when he turns back he smiles and says, 'It's fine. She's cool with it. They're going to nip down to Rugs R Us later and bring you back a Day-Glo Afro.'

Mum tries to whack him playfully with the back of her hand but he dodges the weak blow and says, 'If you're not careful I'll leave you and your wheelchair at the side of the road.'

The second half isn't exactly riveting. Freya turns up late, looking distinctly flustered.

'Sorry, she mutters. 'I was waiting at the bus stop for Jack. Why does he never have any credit on his mobile phone?'

Jesse actually gets more into the game than he had done earlier, but, judging by the amount of time Freya spends shouting at him from the sidelines, he's not having his best match ever. It gets worse when Rottweiler Rubinstein pulls him off ten minutes into the second half, and Duane Mulholland gets a chance to show us what he can do.

Mum can see Jesse is deflated. 'They're one-nil up. I don't know why he's looking so glum,' she says.

As time ticks on, Endymion Road get more desperate and our lot seem to concentrate just that little bit harder. Five minutes from the end, an Endymion Road striker makes a break for it and starts heading for the goal. He's not the fastest runner in the world, but the only thing that stands between him and the keeper is Duane Mulholland. It's dangerous. Duane comes running at the kid and gives a beautiful sliding tackle. Crisis averted. We all mop our brows. Still one-nil.

When the whistle goes, the Joan of Arc boys start bobbing up and down and Duane gets his hair ruffled a lot. I can see this is getting right up Jesse's nose, though he's joining in the celebrations. They're in the finals after all. Jesse's younger and smaller than everyone else on the team and they seem to look upon him as some kind of flukey mascot. Mum blows him little kisses as they dance about and when he rushes over to join us, Uncle Stu says, 'Get yourself shaved and showered, Jesse, and we'll get back home to celebrate.'

That's when I realise that it is our home again. We've squeezed the McLafferty cuckoo out of the nest, even if it is only temporarily – and I don't want her back.

chapter eighteen

The rest of Saturday melts into a kind of crazy fondue of chocolate, champagne and celebration. Uncle Stu nips into an off-licence on the way home saying he's 'seeing a man about a dog' and emerges with a big bag of goodies. There's champagne for the adults, chocolate for me and Jesse – and there's loads of it, Flakes, Aeros, Lion bars, the lot – and it's all to celebrate Joan of Arc's semi-final victory.

Later in the afternoon, Mia and Polly descend on the house like a plague of wig-bearing locusts. Uncle Stu takes this as his cue to buy the food for tomorrow's barbecue, so he disappears off to the supermarket, while Polly and Mia start pulling wigs out of boxes. Mia doesn't seem to think it right that Jesse and I are around for the restyling of our mother's hair, but Mum is adamant we should stay.

'I want to spend as much time with the boys as I can this weekend,' she says, when Mia hints that we might want to make ourselves scarce. 'It's their weekend, too. And anyway, it's not as though they haven't seen the new bald me.'

'You're not bald,' says Mia, 'just thinning.'

'It's only a matter of time,' says Mum, touching her head to check she still has some hair hanging about.

'When we told the woman at Holt Bros why we wanted the wigs, she couldn't do enough for us,' says Polly. 'They were practically falling over themselves to shower us with dodgy wigs, weren't they, Mia? They said just pick out a couple you like and we can take the others back next week.'

Mia nods. She's always been a good friend to Mum, and I sense there's been a bit of jealously creeping in since Polly came on the scene. Polly is quite relaxed around Mum – letting her do what she wants, not fussing too much or pussyfooting around – whereas Mia wants to wrap Mum up in tissue paper and put her away somewhere safe. But today without Mum around, Mia and Polly have obviously been getting on quite well. They even stopped for lunch together.

Polly lays all the wigs out on the bed. There's a red curly wig which even makes Mum smile as it's lifted from the box, a blond Marilyn Monroe, a frumpy brown number and a black bob that's totally Uma

Thurman in *Pulp Fiction*. Mum puts on a long blond wig with a fringe and Mia passes her a mirror. Mum starts laughing.

'Oh, I look like Alice in flipping Wonderland,' she snorts.

'It's fabulous!' laughs Polly.

'Not at my age,' says Mum. 'Queen of Hearts is more my style.'

Polly can't resist the call of the wig and before long she tries on a serious black number that makes her look like a rock chick, and Mia slips a platinum blond beehive over her head. She looks in the mirror and screams.

'Oh my God,' she laughs in mock horror. 'I look like Dusty Springfield's mother.'

They are all swigging champagne now – even Mum has half a glass – and they're starting to giggle.

Polly lifts her glass of champagne and cries, 'Cheers! Here's to good hair days!' and Mum adds, 'Good wig days!' and they all chink glasses and take a swig.

'Come on, you two,' says Polly. 'You're not getting away with it either. If you're joining the Wig Club, you'd better get your hair-don'ts on.'

Jesse sits stony-face in brown curls ('Aw bless, he looks like Shirley Temple,' says Mum) and I've got a punky red number with purple highlights.

'What were you thinking, Polly?' asks Mia. 'That's hardly you, Pat, is it?'

'Well, I rather like it,' says Polly. 'Looks good on you, Lukey. Here.' And she passes me the mirror. I'm not keen on 'Lukey' and when I see my face I'm not so wild about the wig either. I start blushing furiously.

Polly is practically convulsed with laughter. 'Now your face matches your hair,' she screams, and they all cackle away like a coven of sozzled witches. Jesse and I can't help but join in, and soon we're all helpless with laughter and playing musical wigs.

By the time Uncle Stu gets home, laden down with bags, the wigs are back in the boxes ready to be returned to Holt Bros and Mia's messing around with Mum's thin hair.

'I think I'm more of a hat person than a wig person,' says Mum.

'Definitely,' says Mia. 'I'll have a look in the hat department when I take this lot back.'

'Any of that champagne left?' says Uncle Stu.

Polly holds the bottle aloft, then tips it upside down. The smallest of drops escapes.

'Oops,' she says, then gives a loud hiccup. 'All gone.'

The rest of the evening is a rather sober affair (in every sense). Mia and Polly leave together and the four of us just chill out. Mum lies on her bed watching TV, but she seems quiet, miles away. She's looking at the TV, but she's not watching it. She's thinking.

At around three a.m., I can hear Mum calling out. She's calling for Uncle Stu, and when I open the door I can hear voices coming from downstairs.

I want to go down too, but I don't want them to hear me. And I know there are a couple of creaky steps near the bottom that will give the game away. I sit halfway down and listen. The door to the sitting room is ajar and I can hear Mum sobbing.

'I don't want to go back,' she's saying. 'But I don't want to die here. I don't want the boys' last memories to be me, dying, in our home in this room, with some stranger looking after them.'

'I'm here now. I can look after you all,' says Uncle Stu.

'No,' says Mum. 'I don't want that. I don't want my home turned into a hospital. I want to go back.'

'Then I'll stay here with the boys.'

'You've got . . . your own . . . life,' says Mum. She's upset I can tell, but there's something else too. The pain is bad. It's that funny way she breathes that gives it away.

'Have I?' says Uncle Stu. 'What about those kids upstairs? What about their lives, their futures?'

'They're not yours,' says Mum. 'I can't ask that of you. It's too much. They're not your responsibility.'

'So whose responsibility are they? Who's going to look after them? Their father? I don't think so. They need to be here – in their own home, at their own school, with their own friends. It's bad enough losing a parent. They can't lose everything else too.'

'I can't ask you to do that.' Mum's voice is quite low now, but I can still hear what she's saying – just. 'It's not exactly the lifestyle you'd have chosen for yourself, is it Stu? Father of two teenage boys?'

'Oh, I don't know,' he says. 'Could be worse. Always thought I'd make quite a good dad. Frankly, I could do with a change of scene – there's nothing to keep me up north now. Look, Patty, I have a role here, I'll find a new job. It's a whole new start. The boys wouldn't have lasted much longer with that funny old bird, Mrs McLafferty. She's not exactly their favourite pin-up, from what I gather . . .'

'At least they were being looked after,' says Mum. 'I didn't have much choice.'

'I know,' says Uncle Stu. 'But I'm not so sure that McLafferty woman had their best interests at heart. And, Patty, nobody's sat down and told Jesse what's going on yet, and Luke is buckling under the strain of it all.'

'I know I should have told Jesse,' says Mum, and I can't hear the next bit. Her voice is very low and it begins to break.

'I'll have a chat with them separately,' says Stu. 'But I know what you mean about Jesse. I won't spoil his weekend. I'll tell him after you've gone back.'

Mum gives out a little cry.

'I'll get you some more painkillers from the kitchen,' he says.

I quickly retreat up the stairs as I hear him getting up, and I jump back into bed. I lie there counting the cracks in the ceiling and I can feel my heart thumping. It's the first time I really face up to the truth. Mum is dying, she's not going to get better. She's not beating the cancer. It's beating her.

chapter nineteen

'You know what I've forgotten? The charcoal.'

Uncle Stu is standing over a bowl of chicken that he's been marinating. He's gone to great lengths, grating fresh ginger over it, adding a shake of soy sauce, the zest of a couple of limes, and then carefully squeezing out the juice to avoid getting any pips in the marinade. He's been mixing it all up with his bare hands like some kind of manic TV chef, only stopping to grind some salt and pepper over it all.

'There may be some in the shed,' I tell him. 'I'll go.'

'I hope you washed your hands,' Jesse tells him, 'else that's not very hygienic.'

'Oh, and I suppose chucking food all over the kitchen is a much more hygienic way of preparing it, is it?' says Uncle Stu, who's up to his elbows in chicken and marinade. 'Of course I washed my hands, you dope.'

Jesse shuts up. He obviously thought Friday afternoon's fiasco was done and dusted, but it seems all is not forgotten. However, Uncle Stu's not mentioned anything to Mum yet, so I reckon he's not going to tell. Not after last night, anyway.

'Ta-da! Look what I found.'

I come back in, triumphantly holding a bag of charcoal aloft. It looks a bit old and there're some signs of nibbly gnawings going on in the corner, but Uncle Stu seems well pleased.

'Perfect,' he pronounces. 'As long as it burns and gives off heat, we're in business.'

Now he's drizzling honey over the sausages. I'm slightly worried about this – I mean runny honey, sausages? It sounds like something the Teletubbies might knock up in the kitchen. But Uncle Stu gives me one of his sideways glances.

'Sticky sausages,' he announces. 'They're delicious, trust me.'

For once, the weather forecasters haven't been telling porky pies, either. Jesse is playing keepy-uppy at the end of the garden and Mum is sitting contentedly in the sunshine, watching him bounce the ball up and down on his knees. We've wheeled her outside and she's still got an old blanket that Gran crocheted for me when I was a baby draped over her knees to keep her warm, even though the afternoon is beginning to heat up nicely, and she's wearing my NY Mets baseball cap that Uncle Stu bought me for Christmas last year. It looks kind of weird on Mum, but she says it keeps the sun out of her eyes. Polly has arrived and is sitting next to her on an old stool, sipping coffee and recounting some scandalous tale from her Saturday night. Mum is smiling and saying, 'You're terrible you are, Polly,' and Polly is saying, 'Oh, don't you start – I thought you were on my side.'

I've got some history homework that I'm trying to do, but to be honest I'm finding it hard to concentrate on the social changes in Victorian England and it's more for Mum's benefit than mine. She keeps asking me if I'm up to date with everything at school, and, although I tell her yes (which is kind of true), she seems reluctant to believe me. Her eyes look heavy and they keep closing every now and then, as though she's really worn out. Polly stops talking at one stage and tells Mum to 'grab some zeds while I catch up on who's looking skinny in the world of showbiz.' She opens up a copy of *Heat* magazine, and starts flicking through it and tutting in mock horror.

Uncle Stu has certainly gone to town. There's enough food for a whole football team as far as I can see. As well as the chicken, he's done salads and baked spuds, sausages, burgers and bananas wrapped up in bacon to chuck on the barbie.

'Bananas in pyjamas,' he announces proudly. 'They're really good. The bananas go a bit squishy when they're cooked and the bacon gets crispy on the outside.'

'Urgh, sounds disgusting,' I say. 'But I'll take your word for it.'

'Do you want to invite a couple of mates round?' he asks me, as he starts wiping down the kitchen surfaces. 'There's more than enough food to go around.'

'No, you're all right,' I tell him. 'Anyway, Jesse's like a one-man eating machine at the moment. He'll work his way through it all eventually.'

'Must be all that energy he burns up training,' says Uncle Stu. 'They need their calories, these sporty types.'

There's a pause. This seems like a good time while everyone else is out in the garden.

'Uncle Stu,' I say, 'what's going to happen? Is Mum still going back to the hospital later?'

He's standing at the sink with his back to me. He turns around slowly.

'Your mum was always going back tonight, Luke,' he says. 'That's what she wants. It's all arranged.'

'But is Mrs McLafferty coming back? To look after me and Jesse, I mean?'

'No,' says Uncle Stu. 'I'm here now. I'm the one who's going to be looking after you. I spoke to Mrs M this morning and she's staying on at her sister's for a few days. She'll come and get her stuff tomorrow.'

I almost want to jump up and punch the air like Jesse does when they score on the pitch, but it doesn't seem appropriate somehow.

He takes a step closer and says, 'Is that all right by you, Luke?'

'Yeah,' I say. 'It's fine by me.'

Like he hasn't guessed. There's a moment's pause.

'Luke, I know you understand what's wrong with your mum, don't you? You know, about the cancer?'

'Yeah,' I say, trying to sound grown-up and casual about it all. 'Yeah, I know about all that.'

'Jesse doesn't know though, does he?'

'No,' I say, 'he wouldn't understand, Jesse. He only really thinks about football. And occasionally food. I haven't told him yet. Mum didn't want me to.'

Uncle Stu nods.

'That's a big secret for you to carry around, isn't it?'

'It's not a secret from everyone,' I tell him. 'Just Jesse. You know, and Mia and Polly know.'

'Your mum wants him to know now. I promised I'd tell him after the weekend.' Uncle Stu's voice goes a bit quieter. He looks over at the door to the garden.

'Luke, you know your mum's not going to get better, don't you?'

He puts his hand on my shoulder, as though to steady me.

'I'd kind of worked that out,' I say.

'I thought you had,' he says. 'You're a bright kid, Luke. You see, your mum wanted a weekend at home with you guys while she still can. A special weekend . . .'

His voice trails off. I'm not going to fill in the gaps, but I know what he is trying to say next. He swallows hard. I don't think this is easy for him either, but I really don't want to hear the next bit. I pick up the plates and grab the cutlery.

'Then that's what we'll do,' I say. 'Make it special. For Mum. I'll take this stuff outside. Do you think that charcoal is hot enough yet?'

Once we get outside, Uncle Stu starts rattling around among the white-hot charcoal with some barbecue tongs before pronouncing it's ready for cooking.

'I'm starving,' shouts Jesse, running over. 'Can you put the sausages on first, Uncle Stu?'

'Have you done this kind of thing before?' says Polly. 'You look very domesticated in that pinny.'

'Barbecues?' he says, 'Nothing to it. It's all in the preparation, isn't it, Luke?'

When we get going, it's like a little production line. I'm shoving the sausages over to Uncle Stu, he's stuffing them into hot dog buns and handing them to Jesse, who eats them and occasionally passes the odd one on. There's a nice vibe.

Mum says, 'I feel so useless sitting here.' She means 'in this wheelchair' but she doesn't say it. We know what she means.

'Relax,' says Uncle Stu. 'It's all under control. The blokes are in charge today, right, lads? All you girls have to do is stuff your faces with the fruits of our labour.'

'A man who cooks *and* has a sense of humour,' says Polly. 'You'll be telling us you know how to wash up next.'

'Washing up?' he says. 'What's that?'

'Anyone fancy playing "Dodge the Frisbee" when we've eaten?' asks Polly.

'Don't know how to play that,' Jesse mutters through a mouthful of burger.

'Basically, you run round the garden like lunatics and I chuck a frisbee at you. If it hits you, you get to chuck the frisbee.'

'Yeah, sounds cool,' says Jesse with a big cheeseburger grin.

And that's what we do. We eat and we drink and afterwards we run around the garden chucking the frisbee at each other and it's a really good laugh. Jesse throws one too hard and it sails over the fence into old Mr Mankin's garden, and Jesse jumps over the fence to retrieve it. As he's climbing back over, Mr Mankin's dog, Boris, comes bombing up from round the corner where he's been snoozing and barks so hard at Jesse, he almost gives him a panic attack. It's only Polly chucking a sausage up the garden to distract Boris that allows Jesse the time to jump back over. We're laughing so much we all collapse in a huge heap on the lawn.

'I don't think that dog gets enough to eat,' says Uncle Stu. 'Boris was looking mighty hungrily at your bum, Jesse.'

Polly throws another frisbee at Uncle Stu and it whacks him on the side of the head and he chases after her and we laugh some more, and then we notice that Mum has nodded off.

'Let's move Pat into the shade,' says Polly.

So I take the brake off her wheelchair and, as Uncle Stu starts to push her, Mum's eyes open and you can see there's something troubling her.

'Are you all right, Pat?' says Uncle Stu.

'I think I'd better be getting back to the hospital now,' says Mum.

chapter twenty

'I'm sure I'll be fine.' Mum is rubbing her shoulder and grimacing as she touches it. 'I'd best get back, though. Just to be safe.'

She's trying her best to sound casual, but there's some kind of anxiety that's crept into her voice and everyone keeps asking her how she's feeling. We're in the lounge, gathering all her stuff together so that Uncle Stu can drive her back. It's obvious she's in pain and needs proper help. She's twisting a little scrap of blue satin ribbon around her fingers in a strange distracted way. It's as if she's trying to keep her fingers busy to keep the pain at bay, but I don't think it's working.

'Are you coming next weekend too?' says Jesse. 'We could have another barbecue, couldn't we? I liked those pyjama banana things.'

Mum tries her best at a smile, but now she's abandoned the ribbon – it's just fluttered down to the floor – and she's pressing away at her pain relief machine so hard I can see the effort on her face. She beckons Polly over, whispers something in her ear and Polly nods and goes into the hall to make a whispered call on her mobile.

Uncle Stu tells Jesse, 'See, I told you you'd love the barbecue.'

Mum's stuff is packed up by the door. Polly has been rushing around the room like a human whirlwind. Uncle Stu asks Mum if she wants us to call an ambulance, but she says, 'No, no. I don't want all that fuss. You drive me, Stu.'

So here we are, not even forty-eight hours after Mum's homecoming, and she's leaving again. Jesse's standing on the pavement with me and Polly, ready to wave her off. Polly's trying to be very casual about it all, but she's biting her lip anxiously, which is a sure sign this is serious, I reckon. Then her mobile phone goes off and she walks a few metres away from us for another whispered conversation. The suddenness of Mum's departure is even starting to get to Jesse, who's looking a bit bewildered, and I notice that Uncle Stu is doing his best not to make eye contact with us.

'Are you okay to stay with the boys?' he asks Polly. 'I can always drop them at Mia's.'

'No, don't worry, we'll all have a cup of tea and

watch some telly, eh?' says Polly. 'I've spoken to the ward and someone will be there to meet you when you arrive. Just park outside and call them on your mobile – they'll come straight down to help.'

She turns to us and puts on an extra-perky look.

'I can tell you all about the new yoga course I'm thinking of signing up for. It's meant to make you brainier and more relaxed, but I'll settle for firmer thighs and a bit less cellulite, frankly.'

Jesse looks alarmed at the prospect. 'There's a match on the telly this afternoon,' he says quickly. We lean into the passenger door of the car to kiss Mum goodbye.

'Come and see me . . . tomorrow after school,' she says, but it's more of a moan than words now, and there's little gaps and pauses. Her skin is slightly sweaty, slightly damp. 'I'll be feeling better . . . then. Once I'm back.'

Only she isn't. The next day, when I get back from school, it's like the Marie Celeste at home. There's no sign of Uncle Stu, and all Mrs McLafferty's stuff is gone. She's left a note for us on the kitchen table. Well, it's addressed to both of us, but I can tell it's really for Jesse. I don't think she gives a monkey's about me, but then the feeling's kind of mutual. I pass it to Jesse to open.

He starts reading it but he's having trouble with her

slightly shaky old-lady handwriting, it's all loopy and smudgy with big lumpy bits of biro ink, and after the first sentence he passes it to me to decipher. I read it out, but I don't bother with the accent.

Dear Jesse and Luke,

'She's put your name first, even though I'm older. That's typical . . .'

'Just get on with it,' says Jesse.

Sorry to hear your mammy's not feeling any better. Your uncle tells me he's coming to look after you now while she's in the hospital. Well, that's fair enough. What you boys need at a time like this is relatives and some good home cooking. I don't know what your uncle's cooking is like but I know you'll miss me and my casseroles so I've left you a little something for this evening.

Normally I'd ask for at least two weeks' notice, but under the circumstances, beggars can't be choosers.

Yours sincerely,
Bridie McLafferty

'Bridie?' says Jesse. 'That sounds like the Bride of Frankenstein.

'It suits her,' I say.

'What does "beggars can't be choosers" mean anyway?'

'It means,' I explain, 'that she doesn't have any choice.

It's push off, or push off.'

'Look over there,' says Jesse. He nods his head in the direction of the cooker. There's a casserole standing silently on the side. It's an unexploded device, primed to go off at any minute.

'It may be her Irish stew,' he says.

'It may be her liver casserole,' I remind him.

Mrs McLafferty's Irish stew was one of the few dishes in her repertoire we had come to be less afraid of. I can't honestly say we'd grown to love it, but compared to the liver casserole (foul), the hotpot (rank) and the sausage pie ('A lot of sausages suffered in the making of that,' Jack declared one evening when Mrs M had managed to persuade him to stay for supper), it was less of a crime against tastebuds.

'Don't open it,' I tell Jesse as he approaches it, ready to remove the lid and discover what lurks beneath. 'Let's take it straight round to Boris. Make him a very happy dog.'

Half an hour later, the phone rings. It's Uncle Stu. By now Jesse has nipped out for another of his training sessions with Freya.

'You guys okay?'

'Yeah, we're good,' I say. 'I'm watching some children's telly. It's amazing the crap collages you can make with a bit of dried pasta. Jesse's up at the rec with Freya. Any news?'

'I'm still at the hospital,' he says. 'Been here all afternoon.'

'How is she?' I ask. 'Mum said we should come down later.'

I can hear him sigh.

'Yes, that's the problem,' he says. He pauses for a moment. 'Look, she's really not well, Luke. She was in a lot of pain so they've given her extra-heavy-duty painkillers, and they've knocked her out a bit. Now I know you wanted to come down but there's really no point. She's far too drowsy.'

'You coming back?' I ask.

'Yes,' he says. 'I'll be an hour or so, and I'll pick something up for supper on the way. Unless you've eaten already?'

I look over at the sink and see the empty casserole pan. It had indeed turned out to be Mrs McLafferty's liver special. Boris wolfed it down and almost bit my hand off when I tried to get the dish back.

'No,' I tell him truthfully. 'I'm starving.'

Uncle Stu gets back at about seven, about twenty minutes after Jesse. I'm toying around with some geography homework and Jesse's lying exhausted on the sofa. Freya's obviously pushing him hard.

'So how's the training going?' I ask him. Not that I care particularly.

He gives me a very dodgy look.

'Why do you want to know?'

'Just asking,' I say. 'You're taking it all very seriously. I thought your place on the team was all sewn up after the last match.'

'We've seen him down at the rec,' says Jesse, conspiratorially. I haven't a clue what he's talking about. I lean forward as though I'm in on the plot.

'Who?'

Jesse rolls his eyes as if to say, Why do I bother? 'Duane Mulholland.'

'Oh, him,' I say. 'I thought you'd seen him off.'

'He played well on Saturday,' says Jesse. 'He wants my place in the finals, I know he does. Freya reckons she's seen him after school, running around the track with Shav.'

'Shav's sport's mad,' I tell him. He's in my class so I know Shav quite well. 'He's gearing up for the athletics. If Duane's a fast runner, Shav's probably roped him in to that.'

'No,' Jesse shakes his head adamantly. 'Freya agrees. He's doing some serious fitness training. Just because I'm the youngest and a bit on the smaller side, he reckons he can bump me off the team. I know what he's up to.'

'And what are you going to do about it?' I ask. 'If he's better than you, he deserves to play for Joan of Arc.'

'Better make sure he's not better than me then,' says Jesse. He jumps off the sofa as he heads for the back door.

'Dinner in ten,' says Uncle Stu. Twenty seconds later I can hear a thud, thud, thud, Jesse's unmistakable trademark sound of ball being kicked against wall, ball being kicked against wall.

To be honest, I'm finding it hard to concentrate on rift valleys after yesterday, but I manage to get something down on paper while Uncle Stu knocks together what he calls an instant supper – Spanish omelette and oven chips. Afterwards he just collapses in a chair. Jesse and I clean up the kitchen (we're still feeling guilty after Friday's madness) and for once we don't fight. I wash up, he dries and he only smashes one plate, which is pretty good going for Jesse.

'Bet Duane Mulholland wouldn't have dropped that,' I mutter as he bends down to pick up the pieces off the floor.

In the middle of the night, Uncle Stu's mobile goes off. He's got this really annoying ringtone like a hyena cackling, and it's a very quick call because next thing is, I can hear him clumping around, bumping into furniture and jangling his car keys. I wander on to the landing and he's pulling on a sweatshirt.

'Go back to bed,' he whispers, trying not to wake

Jesse. 'I've got to go to the hospital. Your mum's having a bad night.'

'Can I come?' I ask. 'I want to come.'

'No, you stay here with Jesse,' he says. 'I'll send her your love. You've got my mobile number, haven't you? I'll phone you if . . . if I need to,' he says. He ruffles my hair, and points at my room.

'Bed,' he says, in a firm but friendly way. 'I'll be back in the morning to make your breakfast.'

chapter twenty-one

True to his word, Uncle Stu is there in the morning. I couldn't get back to sleep once he'd left, but I must have drifted off just before he came home because I wake up when I hear his key rattling in the front door. One look at the alarm clock tells me it's just gone seven a.m. He heads into the kitchen and I can hear him filling the kettle before he starts calling up the stairs to me and Jesse.

It's weird what goes through your head when you can't sleep. I spent the night thinking back over our weekend, re-running it like a favourite old movie, putting it on slo-mo for the best bits and fast-forwarding through the rubbish. I wished we'd had time to squeeze more in. I kept wondering what was going on and how bad things really were.

One thing I've discovered with adults – you can always rely on them not to tell you the truth when you really want it. They want you to remain kids for ever, in some twisted childhood fantasy. I know Uncle Stu isn't a fully-paid-up member of the Peter Pan brigade, but I also know that he isn't really up to giving me blow-by-blow accounts of what Mum is going through. I suppose he thinks that, though I'm more responsible than Jesse, I still need protecting in some way. That I'm still a kid. Maybe he's right, and I don't want all the gory details. Maybe he's just so knackered after a night spent sitting in a chair next to Mum that he only has enough energy left to pour some cornflakes into a bowl and call it breakfast. Maybe there isn't that much news to share.

So we set off for school together, me and Jesse. It's a bit of a first because we never walk to school together, but we're obviously still in that Blitz mentality. Jesse is quite 'up' because he's got footie practice after school and his mind is obviously stuck in a semi-finals victory groove. He's waffling on about Duane Mulholland again, as if it's the only thing in the world that matters to him, his place on the team. He kicks everything on the way to school as though his place in the squad depends on it. From discarded fag packets to apple cores to old Coke tins, if it'll move, he'll kick it, and in between he's weighing up his talent against Duane Mulholland's. Strangely, it's almost reassuring to hear him twaddling on about something totally unrelated to what's been going on all weekend, but I can't honestly say I'm listening. You know how sometimes you can have a radio on in the background, and someone's talking about the Chancellor and tax rates and you know what it is they're talking about but you're not actually listening? Well, that was our conversation on the way to school. I'd tuned out from Radio Jesse.

When I get to school, the first person I see is Freya.

'Where's Jack?' I ask. Jack is never late for school, and as usual, I've made it with about thirty seconds to spare.

'No show.' She explains. 'It's Tuesday, Luke. Week B.' She looks at me as if I'm daft. 'Sex education? He won't be in today.'

'Oh yeah . . .'

I'd forgotten about that. Jack has a bit of a thing about sex education. While Ms Riley passes round condoms and points at embarrassing anatomical diagrams and the rest of the class collapses in fits of the giggles, Jack can't cope. First his ears go red and then it starts to spread round his face like some awful skin disease. Once, it got so bad that Ms Riley asked him if he felt all right, and of course, that made everybody stare at Jack even more and by the time the bell rang at the end of the lesson he was so puce his face was practically the colour of a Barbie accessory set. It was a bit of a touchy subject and Freya and I weren't allowed to mention it again, ever. And every time we have a double sex education lesson – once a fortnight, week B – he no shows.

Just as I'm about to launch into the business of Uncle Stu getting called out in the middle of the night, Ms Riley starts clearing her throat and asks, 'Now can anyone tell me what they understand by the term "heavy petting"?' and I start to think that maybe Jack has the right idea after all.

We're twenty minutes into the lesson and the embarrassment factor is really kicking in when there's a knock on the classroom door and Ms Riley says, 'Yes?' in that teacherly way and James 'Big Butt' Butterfield waltzes in and says, 'Luke Napier, Miss. Head wants him.'

Ms Riley corrects him by saying 'Ms' very pointedly, but he just raises his eyes to the ceiling and drops them again with a loud 'duh'. I'm thinking, what is it now, what is it now, as I walk to the front. This is getting a little bit too regular for my liking. Jesse's not playing footie till later so he can't have broken anything yet, not unless he tripped on the stairs into class which is always a possibility with Jesse, and then I think, Mum. It just hits me out of nowhere, how can I be so stupid, it's something to do with Mum, and I start to run along the corridor.

'Where you going?' yells Big Butt. 'We've got to get your little brother too, you know.'

I'm running towards Mrs Halloran's office and thinking, 'Please don't let it be *that*.' We've never been that religious in my family – well, not for years, anyway – but I think this is what most people call praying, and that's what I'm doing as I run down the corridor. 'Not that, not that, not yet, please, not yet.'

It becomes a mantra I can't get out of my mind and then I'm outside Mrs H's door, out of breath, and I knock on the door but I'm already opening it as Mrs Halloran says, 'Yes.'

The first thing I see as I open the door is Uncle Stu sitting in the chair opposite Mrs H's desk.

'Luke,' he says, 'I thought . . .'

His voice trails off ominously. Mrs H steps round the desk and puts an awkward arm around my shoulder.

'Your uncle has come to take you and your brother to the hospital, Luke,' says Mrs Halloran. 'It seems your mother's taken a turn for the worse.'

A turn for the worse. What does that mean? It sounds such a bizarre thing to say, as though Mum is some kind of truck veering out of control.

Uncle Stu stands up.

'Come on, we'd best get you and Jesse over to the hospital. She wants to see you both.' He turns away and looks at Mrs Halloran. She's nipped back behind her desk now to protect herself from the real world that's come crashing into her office this morning.

There's a knock at the door and Jesse is propelled into the room by Big Butt.

'What's going on?' he asks as we turn him round and push him back out the door. 'I can't just leave now. I've got football practice this afternoon.'

chapter twenty-two

It's only about fifteen minutes' drive from school to Gospel Park, but it seems much longer than that. We don't say much in the car. It's hard to know what's going on in Jesse's head at the best of times. He may be thinking about missing this afternoon's training session and the likelihood of Duane Mulholland taking his place. I just sit with my nose pressed up against the side window of the car, the world blurring past, until I shut my eyes really tight, hoping that when I open them again I'll suddenly find myself in another life, or at least back in my old one, before everything started to go tits up.

As we leave the car park, Jesse says, 'You've forgotten to pay and display, you'll get a ticket', but Uncle Stu ignores him. We belt our way up the stairs to Spencer ward, Uncle Stu racing ahead, taking two steps at a time. We're getting funny looks from everyone inside because you're not allowed to run in hospitals, but we haven't got time to explain to anyone. When we get to Spencer ward, we go zooming through the doors and past the place where you're meant to wash your hands with the special antiseptic lotion, and there's Mia sitting in a corridor on an orange plastic chair, crying, and Polly is kneeling next to her with her hand around her head. Polly is saying something to Mia very softly, and Mia is dabbing at her eyes with a crumpled-up piece of the blue paper that they use for everything in hospitals.

That's when everything starts to slow down. Everything's been on full tilt for the past half an hour or so, and suddenly the brakes have been slammed on. Mia looks up and sees us, then she stands up saying, 'Luke, Jesse . . .' and she starts to come towards us, holding her arms open wide. It reminds me of a picture of Jesus that Mum had in an old prayer book when we were younger, with fire bursting forth from his sacred heart. She's saying come to me, hold me, I'll comfort you, and I can see she wants comfort too. So we do, we go to her and as we reach her she crumples down to our level and then I hear this awful noise, it's a shuddering, thundering, wailing noise and it's only as she pulls me and Jesse towards her that I realise the noise is coming from me.

Eventually, Mia releases her grip and we come up for

air and she says, 'She's gone, she's gone.' Her cheeks are wet and her eyes are red, and I can see Uncle Stu talking to Polly and she's squeezing his right hand in both her hands and the nurse, Luiz, is coming over to join them and I'm thinking, what happens now, what do we do now?

Uncle Stu is joined by the ward sister who's putting her arm round his shoulder and I can see he's covering his eyes with his hand, and on the other side Polly is stroking his arm.

'Do you want to come and see your mum?' says Mia. 'She just slipped away, really quietly, just a few minutes ago. She was holding on to see you, I could tell, but she didn't have the strength . . .' and then the emotions come bursting through again, like a dam giving way under the strain of it all.

'Yes,' I say, 'I want to see her.'

'I don't know if I want to see a dead person,' says Jesse.

'It's not a dead person,' I say. 'It's our Mum. Don't you want to say goodbye?'

Uncle Stu is standing with us now.

'Come on, boys,' he says. 'Let's all say goodbye together.'

Mia opens the door to the little room at the side and we all go in. The curtain is drawn so there isn't much light but there's a strange perfumed smell. It's then I notice someone's lit a scented candle and placed it beside the bed. I think it's meant to be symbolic, a mark of respect. Mum's lying in the bed, her hands at her side, and she's wearing her old nightie, the one she wears so often when she's sitting at the kitchen table, and I think I'm glad she's wearing that one and not something new that I don't recognise, or one of the hospital's nasty nighties. She looks so quiet and so still and so peaceful. The big furrows on her forehead have all been erased, and I realise of course that's because the pain has gone, it's vanished for ever, and it looks as though our old mum is back.

'She looks beautiful,' says Uncle Stu.

And I don't know why, because I think it's creepy, the idea of touching dead bodies, but she's still my mum and I reach out for her hand, and it's still slightly warm. And I hold it for a minute and say a prayer – that's what she'd have done.

'Do you two want to have a bit of time in here on your own with your mum?' asks Uncle Stu.

'I'd like to go now,' says Jesse. He's looking a bit freaked out round the edges, like it's all been too much for him to take on board in one big gulp.

'Can I stay a minute longer?' I ask, and Uncle Stu nods and guides Jesse out. He carefully leaves the door slightly ajar, and I look back at Mum and the room. I notice the paint is peeling round the top of the ceiling and there's a scuff mark on the wall where someone's shoved the bed too hard, and it all seems such an imperfect world, and yet it doesn't really matter any more, none of it.

I think of all the things I want to tell her. Not just now, I mean, but things I'll want to tell her when I'm older and won't be able to. Like who am I going to moan to if I mess up my GCSE maths, or who am I going to shout at when Jesse starts winding me up? Who's going to help me fill in the form if I want to go to university, and who's going to wash my clothes and match up my socks in pairs in those funny little doughnut shapes, and who's going to make us roast dinners on a Sunday, and what if I get a girlfriend and she's not right for me, who's going to tell me she's not right for me, and I realise I'm crying again now, and I can't say those things because they're all so selfish, they're just about me, and she is lying here dead, and I'm thinking about ME, and that makes me cry even more. It's the same for Jesse, I think, in fact it's worse for him because he's younger and at least I got a couple more years of Mum in than he did. I hold her hand tighter and squeeze it harder and I can't stop crying now. It's all coming down and I just blurt out, 'Oh Mum, why d'you have to go and die?'

chapter twenty-three

It's funny, but I had a teacher in Year Three called Miss Tranter and she was one of those wise teachers who said things that got stuck in your brain and you just carry them around with you for ever. She once told us that we should never be afraid to put up our hands if we didn't understand anything for fear of sounding stupid. What started it all was this girl called Josie Pegg who had thrown her lunch out after Miss Tranter had told us to take everything out of our desks that didn't come under the category 'books' and chuck it in the big plastic bin in the corner. As Josie stood in tears gazing at her ham sandwiches covered in cack, Miss Tranter said it was a shame to do something wrong just because you were afraid to ask. The lesson I learned was, it's not so dumb to ask if you're not sure about stuff.

It's about three days after Mum has gone (people don't

like to use the word 'died', I've noticed, and it seems to have rubbed off on me) and Polly has come round our house to see how we're getting on. I suspect this is beyond the call of duty, but that's Polly for you.

She hasn't changed a bit in the way she speaks to us. We have had a constant stream of visitors – friends of Mum's, Freya and Jack, even Mrs Halloran (that was very embarrassing) – and everyone who comes to the house is saying things like, 'I'm so sorry' and, 'If there's anything we can do to help', and I really want to say, 'Well, yes, there is actually. How about bringing my mother back to life?' I have stupid thoughts like that all the time, but of course, you don't say anything, you just nod and smile. But Polly's been brilliant.

We haven't got a clue what to do. Jesse and I just sit like a couple of morons on the sofa, gazing into space. We're off school at the moment – Uncle Stu says we don't have to go in until after the funeral – but doing ordinary everyday stuff seems a bit disrespectful right now.

Polly says, 'You can turn the telly on if you want, you know.' Then, as if she is reading Jesse's mind, she tells him, 'I think you could do with some fresh air, Jesse. Why don't you have a bit of a kick-around in the garden, eh?'

Jesse tries his best not to break out in a big smirk as he practically flies out of the back door. It's the first time he's touched a ball since last weekend.

Once he's gone, Polly gets up and closes the door. Uncle Stu is off making arrangements for Monday, the day of the funeral, and she sits next to me on the sofa. I can smell her funny fruity perfume, which is strangely reassuring, and she picks up the remote for the telly and turns it down a few notches, but she doesn't turn it off. It's the news and they're talking about a famine somewhere in central Africa, and I'd love to switch channels as I see these images of children with big swollen heads and flies landing all over their lips, but I don't.

'Luke, I have to talk to you about the funeral,' she says. 'Stu's got a lot on his plate at the moment and I said I'd help out, but I don't really know what to do about your dad.'

She leaves a pause for me to step in.

'What about him?' I say.

To be honest, I have thought about him a bit since Tuesday, which is a lot more than I've thought about him in the past six years or so. Usually it is when I'm feeling a bit sorry for myself. I mean, some kids in my class have got two parents. Look at Freya. Her mum and dad both work and they've got two cars and a big house, and I know it's a bit untidy sometimes, but whenever you go round there, Angela's really nice and asks you to sit down and makes you tea and toast and chats. And I know David's a bit grumpy and he grunts and bumps about the house like a big grizzly bear and he never looks like he's pleased to see you, but Freya always says, 'Take no notice, that's just David.' And, even though he doesn't say much, I've seen her give him the odd hug and you can tell she really loves him.

Well, I never felt cheated only having one parent because, well, who needs two if you've got one really good one? Dad just didn't come into the equation. He was off and away and it's not like we missed him or he sent us money (I overheard Mum telling Mia once, but she never moaned about it to me and Jesse) or anything useful like that. We had Mum so we didn't even think about it.

'Stuart's obviously spoken to your dad,' says Polly, 'and Ian would like to come down for the funeral. On his own. He won't bring his wife and kids – he realises that that's not appropriate – but he says he wants to pay Patty his last respects.'

Ian, I think. I'd forgotten that was his name. Ian. I try to put a face to the name, but it's a big blur nowadays.

'Does it make any difference if I say no?'

Polly smiles at me, and picks up my hand and gives it a little squeeze.

'Of course it does,' she says. 'That's why I'm asking. It's up to you and Jesse. Stuart says he never had anything against Ian. Marriages break up, these things happen. But he realises that Monday is going to be tough on both of you two. If seeing your dad makes it even harder to take, he'll ask him not to come. And your father says he'll respect that.'

She leaves another gap here, but I'm still too busy thinking to say anything.

'He doesn't have to come back to the house after the funeral if you don't want him to, you know.'

I take a big deep breath and look at the telly.

The TV reporter is standing next to a group of children who all look seriously skinny, like they're on the brink of death, really. I'm wondering if TV news reporters feel guilty when they sit down and eat their dinner after they've told the rest of the world about a country that's gripped by starvation. I'm also thinking, come on, Luke, you may have your problems but at least you have enough to eat and your head's not covered in manky flies.

It's then that I think of the Miss Tranter question that's been on my mind and I think, I have to ask it or I may end up looking stupid, like Josie Pegg staring at those ham sandwiches in the bin with bits of fluff and pencil shavings stuck to them.

'Polly,' I say, 'why did it happen to us? I mean, how come Jesse and I have ended up with no parents and some people have two. It's not exactly fair is it?'

Polly closes her eyes briefly and then she stares right at me. 'Luke,' she says. 'It's never easy when someone dies. You start to question all kinds of things. I see that a lot – people asking, "Why me?" There's no answer. I could start spouting all kinds of clichés, but I don't know if they would make you feel any better right now. You're not being punished, you know. It's not like you deserve this. And it's not because your mum did some awful things in her life. I only knew Pat a few weeks, but you didn't have to be a genius to see what a strong, funny, lovely person she was.'

'I keep wondering if we could have done more,' I tell her. 'If Mum hadn't come home that weekend, well, maybe she'd still be alive now.'

Polly takes a slow, deep breath. 'Of course you'll think that. It's perfectly natural. Look, Luke, the doctors at Gospel Park are fantastic. Yes, they knew your mum's cancer was advanced, but they didn't realise just how advanced it was, and nor did she. She still thought she had some time. There were still things she wanted to do – she hadn't even had time to talk to Jesse about the cancer – but suddenly her illness just kicked into overdrive. That happens sometimes, but it's unusual, you know, it's very rare. The recovery rate for cancer nowadays is better than it's ever been. People do survive, they do get better, but a few don't. Maybe that last weekend was a bit much for Pat, but do you know what? I don't think she'd have traded it for another two weeks in her hospital bed. And I don't think you and Jesse would either.'

She looks me straight in the eyes. I know Polly's

right. I know this all makes sense.

'It's the law of nature, Luke. We all have to die. Some of us die sooner than others. The best thing we can do is make the most of it while we can.'

She smiles. 'And I said I wasn't going to give you all those old clichés . . .'

She's still staring right at me, and I'm thinking that she's got a really friendly, caring face.

'Live, Luke. Enjoy it. Don't waste your time feeling angry or hard-done-by, or let down, because your mum's gone and your dad's moved on. You've got friends – good friends – you've got an uncle who loves you and who's going to look after you. You've got a brother, too, and I know you think he's a pain now but that won't last for ever. Your dad may not have been much of a father to you recently, but who knows,' she says, 'one day, that might all change, too.'

The news has moved on from the starving African children. Now they're talking about some changes to the tax system that the government is proposing. In a few minutes, no doubt they'll be finishing up with a tap-dancing dog to make us all feel chirpy.

'I don't mind if he comes,' I say. 'I don't really know him. I'll ask Jesse but I don't think he'll care either way.'

Polly squeezes my hand again and says, 'Good. I think that's very honest of you. I'll tell Stuart.'

chapter twenty-four

I don't know how the word 'fun' ended up in funeral, but personally I think someone has a very sick sense of humour.

Uncle Stu has been talking to us about the funeral – I think Polly suggested it might be a good idea – so we're not in for any nasty surprises on the day itself. It seems he and Mum had talked about it at some length a few days before she died, and she had made a few special requests (typical Mum).

1) She wanted it in the local church, the Holy Cross.

2) She wanted the nice South American priest who baptised Jesse – Father de Freitas – not the doddery old codger who's always banging on about eternal damnation and shakes the collection plate under your nose a second time on the way out of church (she always said that was the reason why we stopped going).

3) No gloomy hymns, only happy ones.

4) No wearing black (she said it reminded her of funerals – work that one out).

5) She wanted to be buried, not cremated.

6) No flowers.

I'm slightly perplexed by this last request. I mean, it's not as though she didn't like flowers – she loved them. For Mother's Day last year Jesse and I clubbed together and bought her some anemones from the flower shop up the road. We bought anemones because we liked the colours and we couldn't afford the roses. Mum said she was glad we didn't get the roses (Jesse blurted out that they were too expensive) because she always thought they were 'lacking in imagination'. I think this was a reference to my dad who always bought her a bunch of moth-eaten roses from the local petrol station every Valentine's Day and thought this qualified as a grand romantic gesture. Mum didn't see it quite the same way. She also said anemones were her favourites. Okay, maybe she said it just to make us feel better, but we believed her at the time. And I found one of the purple anemones that she'd squashed in her memory book (it was where she kept her favourite photos and little mementoes), and she'd written next to it *Mother's Day 2008*, so I think it did mean something to her.

I tell Uncle Stu I really want to get her some anemones even though she'd said no flowers and he says that's cool because 'no flowers' means people outside the immediate family, but we can still get flowers if we want. He says Mum thought it a shame that beautiful flowers just end up wilting in a cemetery with no one to look at them. He also says he'd like to ask people who would have spent money on flowers to make a donation to Cancer Research and Macmillan nurses instead, if Jesse and I agree (we do).

'Can they make flowers into special shapes?' asks Jesse.

'Like what?' I say. 'The Titanic? The Sydney Opera House? Your brain?'

'I was thinking that Mum might like a football,' says Jesse quietly.

I practically choke.

'You mean you might like a football,' I say. 'It's not for you. It's for Mum.'

'Yes, but she liked to watch me play,' says Jesse. My jaw drops open. This is news to me. I remember the time when she watched him play at primary school on a freezing Saturday in February and she claimed the experience had left her with chilblains on her left foot and frostbite on her right.

'Sometimes she did,' he adds under his breath.

'I think a wreath in the shape of a football would be perfect,' says Uncle Stu. 'I'll see what the florist can do.'

I hear him on the phone to the florist later when Jesse is outside again, kicking the ball against the wall.

Mum may have died, but Jesse obviously still has the finals of the Inter-County Schools Under-16s on his mind. Or maybe it's the World Cup 2018.

'I know it's unusual,' Uncle Stu is hissing down the phone, trying hard not to raise his voice, 'but it's what my nephew has requested. He's only ten, and his mother's died. Is it really too much to ask to try and make a little boy happy?'

It's funny how adults can be economical with the truth about your age. Like when you go to a theme park and they tell you to say you're eleven if anyone asks when you know perfectly well you're twelve. Of course Jesse's not ten (though he acts like it sometimes), but adults like to age you up or down to suit their own ends. As though a florist wouldn't mind breaking the heart of a bereaved almost-twelve-year-old, but wouldn't dream of saying no to a distraught ten-year-old.

He gets his way in the end though. Well, it's hardly surprising. 'They didn't want to do it?' I say as Uncle Stu comes into the kitchen to make a cup of coffee.

'Oh, they say it's a nightmare trying to get black and white flowers to make it look like a football,' says Uncle Stu. 'Well, they can get white flowers – it's the black ones that are the problem. I told them to use red.'

I give him a look that says 'are you sure about that?'

'I've seen kids at the park kicking red and white footballs,' says Uncle Stu defensively. 'It's meant to be

174

a bloody gesture, not the FA Cup Final.'

We both snigger at this, and then I say, 'Jesse won't mind. Red and white – they're his colours, aren't they?' and Uncle Stu nods his head to show he understands.

He says he's going to say a few words about Mum at the funeral and asks if I want to say something too. I can't think of anything I'd less like to do except possibly insert hot needles under my fingernails. I figure if I can get through the ceremony without falling to pieces it will be a major achievement and I'm really not keen on the idea of standing up in front of a whole church full of people and putting on a bit of a performance. So I say, 'Thanks but I don't think it's my style,' in as firm and tactful a voice as I can manage, and Uncle Stu is cool about that.

'Why don't you write her a poem?' he suggests. 'Your Mum always said you were good at that. You don't have to read it out, but we could put it with your flowers on the coffin, so it's private.'

I must admit, I like this idea. I spend the rest of the day trying to get some words on to paper but it's not as easy as I'd thought. Trouble is, if it's a rhyming type of poem it reads like something out of those really naff birthday cards you get at the local newsagent, or, worse still, brings back horrible memories of the carnage that was 'Hyacinth Wood'. And if it's the non-rhyming kind, it seems a bit pretentious somehow. I have a go at both and then go back to the rhyming sort. I want to find something that rhymes with my name so I can sign it off, but the only thing that rhymes with Luke is 'puke' and even I can tell that that is 'far from appropriate' as Mrs Blythe would say. Eventually I settle for this.

If I close my eyes
I can hear your voice
Above the sound, the background noise.
I can hear your laughter
Loud and clear
And I wish you weren't gone, Mum
I wish you were here.

I'm trying to think of a title, but that turns out to be even more difficult than writing the poem in the first place. Then I remember what Mum used to write at the end of postcards when we went away on holiday. *Wish you were here.* So I scrawl that across the top and I look at it for a bit. It feels right, it seems to fit somehow. Wish you were here.

I go rummaging through my desk upstairs and find some blue marbled writing paper that I got in my Christmas stocking last Christmas (she'll know where it came from) and I write it out with my fountain pen in really neat handwriting. It's not an epic, but it takes me a few attempts to get it just right. The fountain pen is a bit leaky, because I don't use it that often, and writing with a fountain pen is obviously a bit of an art. I manage to smudge the first couple of goes, just because I'm trying a bit too hard, but eventually I get a little system where I write then blot, then write, then blot, and eventually I get it just the way I want it. Then I put it in one of the matching blue marbled envelopes, write 'Mum' on the front, and stand it up on the mantelpiece. Then I have to admit I have a bit of a boo because I get to thinking I'll never write 'Mum' on another envelope again.

Polly comes round later and cooks pasta for supper. While we're twirling spaghetti bolognese around our forks, she asks, 'Have you thought if you'd like to say anything at the funeral, Jesse?'

He slurps up a string of spaghetti, leaving tomatoey trails around his mouth as he sucks it in. This is Jesse thinking.

'Yes,' he announces. 'I think I want to read a poem.'

'Good for you,' says Polly. 'Have you got anything in mind or would you like some help?'

'I wouldn't mind some help,' he says. 'I'm not very good with poems. But I don't want anything too mushy.'

'Luke's good with poetry,' says Uncle Stu. 'He'll give you a hand.'

'No I won't,' I say. This is guaranteed to make me look bad, if he reads and I don't – especially as I'm older than him.

'I've got a book of poems for funerals,' says Polly. 'We can have a look through after supper and see if there's anything there you fancy.'

Jesse seems to like this idea. As he takes his plate to dump it in the sink, Polly turns to me.

'Luke, we all do our own thing. We all grieve in our own ways. Don't feel bad if Jesse wants to say something in the church and you don't. It's totally cool. We all know you've written Patty a poem and it's private. I think that's lovely.'

'Right,' Uncle Stu says to me. 'That's you and me on washing-up duty while the poets get stuck in.'

'Most of these are long and boring,' proclaims Jesse, as though he's some kind of poetry expert now. 'I can't even say some of the words.'

'They're all a bit serious,' Polly agrees. 'And some are a little bit on the morbid side.'

Jesse nods in agreement, then says, 'What's morbid mean?'

'It's means they're all obsessed with death,' Polly explains.

'Which seems stupid when you're already at a funeral,' says Jesse. 'Of course it's all about death. Duh! I don't want anything mobid.'

'Morbid,' Polly corrects him. 'Okay, let's go for

cheerful and uplifting then, shall we?'

But the more they read, the more depressing the poems seem to get.

'Why don't you read something that you liked at school?' says Uncle Stu, standing in the doorway, drying a saucepan with a tea towel. 'Something you associate with your mum. Something that made her happy.'

'I know!' says Jesse and he runs upstairs to his room. He emerges a few minutes later with an old exercise book.

'What do you think of this?' he says. 'I read it out for class assembly in Year Four and Mum said it made her cry.

The Owl and the Pussy-Cat went to sea
In a beautiful pea-green boat.
They took some honey, and plenty of money,
Wrapped up in a five-pound note.
The Owl looked up to the stars above,
And sang to a small guitar,
"O lovely Pussy! O Pussy, my love,
What a beautiful Pussy you are,
You are,
You are!
What a beautiful Pussy you are!"

'It was my favourite poem,' says Jesse, holding up the dog-eared exercise book. 'Look, I even drew a picture of the Owl and the Pussy-Cat.'

He passes the book to Uncle Stu.

'You don't think it's too babyish, do you?'

'I think it's perfect,' he says. 'And if your mum loved it, that's all the more reason to read it out.'

'Yes!' says Jesse, punching the air as though he's scored a winning goal.

chapter twenty-five

'What's he look like?' says Jesse. 'Is he that tall spotty bloke over there?'

We're standing outside the Holy Cross church, and Jesse's craning his neck round the pillars in the church porch, trying to work out which one is our father (not the one who art in heaven, the one who art down here on earth). He's pointing at one of the hospital porters who must be about eighteen.

'No,' I say patiently. 'I can't remember what he looks like, but it's definitely not him. That's Joe who works at Gospel Park.'

'Oh yes,' says Jesse, screwing up his eyes. 'I thought I recognised him.'

'No, you didn't,' I say. 'We've talked to Joe loads of times. He always used to give us chewing gum when Mum wasn't looking.'

Jesse is screwing up his eyes. He probably needs glasses.

I'm not altogether sure our dad has shown up after all. Trouble is, there are a lot of people we don't know, so he could be any one of a number of possible suspects.

The church is packed and after the service everyone empties out slowly on to the forecourt at the front where the hearse is waiting. Nobody rushes round at funerals, I discover. Everyone takes their time. Uncle Stu is walking about kissing and hugging people, saying, 'Thank you for coming' and, 'Are you coming back to the house afterwards?' and shaking hands. Most of the crying seems to have stopped now, although I can still see the odd Kleenex being dabbed about. I'm worried for a moment that Mrs M might have turned up, but I scan the congregation and can't see any sign. She's probably busy knitting tea-cosies or whatever it is she gets up to during the day. A couple of undertakers are loading the coffin on to the hearse, and Jesse's football is propped up beside it, next to a posy of anemones with my poem attached. There's a big pearly-ended steel pin piercing the envelope that's been impaled through the middle of the flowers, binding the two together.

It got a bit hairy in the church at one point. Uncle Stu was giving a speech about Mum (his eulogy as he had been calling it for the past few days) and he was just saying that 'her sunshine smile warmed all our lives' when he started getting choked up. He almost went into emotional meltdown, but he stopped a moment, cleared his throat, took a deep breath and finished his piece before returning to his seat. I wanted to clap but I didn't think it was the done thing in churches, and probably never at funerals. As he sat down, Polly, who was seated to his left, rubbed his arm as if to say, 'You did well' and, 'Phew, that's over' all in one, and Uncle Stu reached out for Jesse's hand (he was sitting on the other side). Then the next hymn started up. It was Jesse's choice.

Bearing in mind that Mum had said she didn't want anything too gloomy, he'd chosen 'Kum Ba Yah'. Now I have a sneaking suspicion that Mum couldn't stick 'Kum Ba Yah'. I seem to remember on one occasion when we were in church and 'Kum Ba Yah' kicked in, complete with acoustic guitar and tambourine accompaniment, she sighed loudly and said, 'Not that ruddy hippy anthem' under her breath, but Jesse was singing away like the clappers (he reckons they sing it sometimes on the terraces at matches but they change the lyrics to something less godly), so I just shut up and sang along, if that's not a contradiction. I've still got no idea what it means. Probably something filthy in Swahili.

Freya comes up to me and gives me a big hug from behind while Jack skulks around us. Both sets of parents are hovering on the sidelines, and Freya's wearing a canary-yellow sundress and a pair of gold ballet pumps. It's so bright I almost wish I was wearing sunglasses, but not like the ones Freya is wearing. They're huge pink stars that cover half her face. 'You look very, er . . . summery,' I say.

'Well, I thought this was meant to be a celebration,' says Freya. 'You distinctly told me your mum said no black.'

She raises an eyebrow, and looks at my jacket accusingly.

I'm wearing a smart jacket that Uncle Stu and I bought from Top Man two days ago. I've never had a smart jacket before and I'm thinking we really should have got the bigger size as it's pinching a bit under the arms, but I don't suppose I'm going to wear it again anyway. It's not exactly going to conjure up happy memories. I suppose I could always drag it out of mothballs for work experience if I get desperate and I manage not to grow in the next year.

'It's blue,' I say, 'not black. It's navy blue.'

Freya gives me one of her sideways glances that says 'same difference' but she doesn't take it up again. Jack is wearing his parka which looks a little out of place at this time of year, but at least he hasn't got the hood up.

'Are you coming to the cemetery?' I ask. Jack looks at Freya.

'She is. I'm not,' he says.

'Right,' I say.

'Cemeteries kinda freak me out,' says Jack. 'You know, vampires and that . . .'

I can see Freya grinding a gold ballet pump into his toe and Jack says 'ow' a little too loudly in his cross voice.

'I'll come,' she says, 'if that's all right with you? I'll leave David and Angela here to make their own way home, though.' She looks over her shoulder. Freya's parents smile sympathetically. They look a bit lost, as though they're desperate to get away. 'They'll only get . . .' she pauses, ' . . . upset.'

I nod.

As we're climbing into the back of this super-sized Seventies Daimler, Freya scans the horizon like a bird of prey and whispers, 'Which one's your dad?'

I whisper back, 'I can't really remember. He did leave six years ago, you know.'

'Well, you must have some photos of him knocking around the house.'

'Mum burnt them all,' I explain. 'Well, I think she scratched his face out first, then ripped them up, and then burnt them.'

'Ooh,' says Freya, drawing in her breath dramatically. 'Sounds acrimonious to me.'

'There's loads of room in here,' says Jesse. For once he's right. I imagine in some parts of the world whole families inhabit a space a fraction of this size.

'Is Dad here, Uncle Stu?' Jesse asks.

'Yes, he's here,' says Uncle Stu. 'He was sitting a few rows behind us.'

'He could have said something to us,' says Jesse. 'It's not very friendly, just ignoring us like that.'

'Hey, come on,' says Uncle Stu. 'It's a bit tricky right now. I'll call him over after the . . .' he pauses, and his voice goes all quiet, '. . . interment.'

'The what?' says Jesse.

'Burial,' says Freya. 'After the burial.'

'Oh, okay,' he says.

And he does. We're walking away from the grave, like a school snake of mourners. There's Mia and Andy walking beside me, and Uncle Stu is next to me and Jesse's on the other side. Polly and Luiz have come too, and they're walking behind us with Freya, and there are more friends of Mum, some of whom go back years that I remember her talking about but I've never actually met.

Uncle Stu is looking a bit spaced out, but I suppose he's had a lot to take in. Polly skips up behind him as we approach the cemetery gates where the big black vulture of a Daimler is waiting to fly us back home, and she hooks her arms through mine and Uncle Stu's.

'It's like the Batmobile,' says Jesse.

Polly rubs Uncle Stu's shoulder.

'You look as though you need a drink,' she says.

Suddenly, Jesse remembers and starts shaking Uncle Stu's sleeve.

'Which one is he? Our dad?' he demands.

Uncle Stu turns round and puts his hand up against the sun and I can see a man walking on his own, slightly apart, smoking a cigarette. And now I look at him, there is something familiar about this bloke, the way he walks, some sort of memory that seems to be rising up to the surface. He looks shorter than I remember somehow – though he's about six foot – and a bit older, but as I haven't seen him for years that's not surprising. He's got floppy sandy-coloured hair, a bit like Jesse I suppose, and as he looks up he sees Uncle Stu pointing him out to us, and we three start walking towards him.

'Hello, Stuart,' he says to Uncle Stu, holding out his hand to him. 'Good to see you. Well, I mean, sorry it's not happier circumstances . . .'

'Ian,' says Uncle Stu in acknowledgement, taking his hand and shaking it.

Dad (seems weird calling someone you hardly know 'Dad') takes a drag on his cigarette, then flicks it away.

'Thought I'd given those up,' he says in a soft

Scottish drawl. 'First thing you reach for when you get bad news, isn't it?'

He looks at me. I'm thinking, he's got a Scottish accent. It doesn't sound that Scottish when he phones.

'How are you, Luke? All right?'

It's not a stupid question really, he's just talking to fill the gaps.

'Do you remember me?' Jesse pipes up, shielding his eyes from the sun as he looks up at him.

'Of course I do,' says Dad. 'I was there when you were born, you know. Both of you.'

'Haven't been around much lately though,' I say. I didn't mean it to come out like that – it sounds really hostile and bitter – and he looks at me and does a sort of smiley-sighy thing, and says, 'No. No I haven't.'

'Will you come back to the house for a drink?' says Uncle Stu.

'I'd love to,' says Dad, 'I could do with a drink. But I've got to get the train back, Stuart. Jasmine's working tomorrow and I'm looking after the kids.'

He means his other family, his real kids. We're his old life, the one that doesn't count any more.

'I'll call you for a chat next week, lads,' he says. 'Find out how you're going, how things are settling down.'

'Yeah,' I say. 'That'll be nice.'

Yeah, I'm thinking. That'll be the day.

'We're in the finals,' says Jesse. He seems desperate

to make some kind of connection with this bloke. The man-formerly-known-as-Dad gives him a gormless look that says, 'I haven't got a clue what you're going on about.'

'Football,' says Jesse by way of explanation.

'You playing for the school team, now?'

Jesse nods proudly.

'We're in the finals,' he repeats.

'That's great,' he says. 'I'll want to hear all about it next week when I call.'

We're just outside the cemetery gates now, and we have to get into the Deathmobile to take us home. I suppose we could offer him a lift to the station – the car's big enough – but we don't. I don't really feel like it's my place to do the offering, and I think Uncle Stu has other things on his mind. I think he's fretting about whether the two catering packs of sausage rolls he bought yesterday are going to be enough to go round.

Dad says, 'Bye then' and starts walking away from us, towards the station, reaching inside his pocket for his mobile phone. Or maybe another fag.

'Do you think he'll call?' asks Jesse.

'Oh, I reckon he will,' I say. 'Five minutes next week then we won't hear from him again till Christmas.'

'What are you up to tomorrow, Jesse?' asks Freya, who's coming back with us in the car. 'You've had a good break from training now. It's time to get back on the horse.'

'What horse?' says Jesse. 'We're not riding, are we?'

'No, we're not riding,' says Freya. She's always quite patient with Jesse. He's one of the youngest in his year and he's not always the sharpest knife in the drawer. Unless you're counting players or comparing league tables, in which case he's as quick as a calculator. 'That's just a saying. We're jogging tomorrow morning, and practising turns. Seven-thirty at the rec. If you're late you'll do double press-ups.'

Jesse doesn't say anything. I don't suppose today's been easy for him, and he's not done any training with Freya since Mum died.

'I saw Duane Whatsit at the rec the other day,' says Freya, casually. 'Running with Shav, he was. Getting a bit speedy, I'd say.'

She turns away and looks out of the window. I like her style.

'Seven-thirty,' says Jesse. 'I'll be there.'

chapter twenty-six

'Get off me now!'

I'm kneeling on top of Jesse's chest, desperately trying to hold his arms down while he's thrashing about, doing his best to topple me.

He's red in the face and looks like he's ready to burst, like an overripe tomato.

'Sod off, you big bully!'

Uncle Stu suddenly comes bursting into the lounge, hauling me off my brother.

'Okay, okay, time out, lads,' he says, as he deposits me on the sofa. He's quite strong, is Uncle Stu. Because he manages to pull me up with one arm and keep Jesse where he is with the other.

'What was it this time?'

Jesse is crying now in fury – he hates it when I pin him down – and he's got snot hanging out of his nose as he gets up. Disgusting. He starts trying to wipe it away on the sleeve of his grey school jersey, and he snivels as he wipes.

'It's Luke. He's picking on me again,' says Jesse. 'He's always having a go at me. It's not fair.'

He's really bawling now, and I can tell he's about ready to blow his top.

'Why don't you leave me alone, you . . . you . . . bastard!' he screams and runs out of the room and up the stairs.

Uncle Stu looks at me and sighs.

'Well, I'm glad you two are getting on so well,' he says. 'What was it about this time, Luke?'

'He wouldn't give me the TV remote,' I explain. 'He knew I wanted to watch *Hollyoaks*. He's just winding me up constantly.'

This is true, I tell myself. He's always trying to rile me, talking about his stupid football and singing his silly soccer songs and trying to hog the remote when it's my turn to watch the telly. I've almost convinced myself.

'Arguing over a daft soap, for God's sake,' says Uncle Stu. 'You don't even like *Hollyoaks*, Luke. You've got to get along, you two. I was going to go out tonight, but I can't exactly leave you on your own if you're going to start killing each other.'

Uncle Stu looks at me. It's been two weeks since the funeral and I can see him thinking, I shouldn't have said that.

'It's all right,' I say. 'You don't have to get

embarrassed every time you mention death or dying or killing, you know.'

'Oh, it's not very sensitive of me,' says Uncle Stu, sitting down next to me on the sofa and running his fingers through his hair. 'You and Jesse have just lost your mother and I seem to have the happy knack of raking up death every five minutes.'

'It doesn't matter,' I tell him. 'And I'm sorry about the fighting. I suppose it's our way of saying we're back to normal.'

'Normal?' he says, sounding exasperated. 'If bashing seven shades of shit out of each other is normal then God help us. I am trying to get a job at the moment, you do realise? If I'm working during the day, I'm not going to be around when you two get home from school. I don't fancy wiping up bits of bone and blood off the carpet every night, thanks very much.'

'How did your interview go today, Uncle Stu?' I ask him.

He gives me the sideways look. This reminds me of Mum, but I'm not going to mention that. It's his way of saying, I realise that's a not-very-subtle subject swerve but I'm going to ignore it. I figure they were quite alike, Mum and Uncle Stu. I wish I'd seen them together a bit more, but it wasn't easy with him being up in Manchester.

'Listen, kiddo,' he says, 'I think it's time you dropped the "Uncle".'

I look at him, alarmed. What's he mean, drop the 'Uncle'? What are we meant to call him? Mum?

'Now I'm looking after you,' says Uncle Stu, 'I think we can be a little less formal, don't you? It's Uncle Stu this, Uncle Stu that, every five minutes. Which is fine. But you two aren't kids any more, and I'm not exactly the Werthers Original type.'

I see his point. The constant Uncle Stu-ing was starting to irritate me too, to be honest. Somehow it doesn't sound so bad when you're tacking 'Mum' on to the end of every sentence, but 'Uncle Stu' is a bit of a mouthful.

'What do you want us to call you?' I ask. Please God, don't let it be 'Dad', I'm thinking.

'Well, obviously nothing obscene,' he jokes. 'Stuart. Stu, if you're feeling friendly. It is my name, you know.'

'Okay,' I nod in agreement. 'On one condition. Stu.'

'What's that?' he says. 'Luke.'

'You drop the "kiddo".'

He laughs and holds out his hand.

'Deal.'

To celebrate the passing of Uncle Stu and the arrival of Stu, he makes us his special spaghetti and meatballs which Jesse describes as one of his All-Time Top Five Suppers. While we're eating, Stu tells us about his latest plan that actually sounds quite sensible. It seems the good news is, Mum had a life assurance policy that she paid regularly every month, so we don't have a mortgage on our house any more. It also means that one day the house will belong to me and Jesse (I'm trying not to think about the inevitable rows that'll cause).

The bad news is, we still need money to pay the bills, buy food, go on holiday, etc. So Uncle Stu, sorry, Stu (this'll take a bit of getting used to) says he's got a master plan. He'll do a bit of temporary translation work to earn some cash and enrol at teacher training college. He says he was thinking about teaching before all this happened in any case. He's got a degree, so it's only one year's training, and then they'll let him loose on unsuspecting mugs like me and Jesse. He reckons they're crying out for good language teachers and all I know is he can't be any worse than our Spanish teacher, Ms Formby, who seems fairly clueless about what day of the week it is, never mind Spanish. Stu says he's also picked up a bit of Cantonese on his travels and, if he does evening classes to brush that up, it may come in very handy. He ends by reading us the riot act and telling us he's off out to see some mates.

'Where *are* you going?' says Jesse as Stu comes downstairs. He's put wax in his hair and he's changed his shirt.

'Who are you, my social secretary?' says Stu. 'Out.'

'That's what teenagers are meant to say, not

responsible adults,' I point out.

He taps the side of his nose. 'When you get older, I promise you I'll respect your privacy too,' he says. 'In the meantime, no arguing, no fighting and no setting fire to your farts or the house. If you do need me in an emergency, you can call me on this.'

He holds his mobile phone aloft as he opens the front door. 'It's called a mobile phone. Very useful things they are, too.'

'Will you be back before we go to bed?' asks Jesse.

'I bloody hope not,' he says. 'It's school tomorrow for you two. Jesse, bed at nine-thirty p.m. and Luke, you can stay up till half-ten. If either of you is still up by time I stagger in, I'll show you what fighting really is.'

As he closes the door Jesse says, 'That's if he's back at all, of course.'

'What's that supposed to mean?' I ask.

'Well, it's obvious,' says Jesse. 'He stinks of aftershave. He's gone on the pull.'

I chuck a cushion at him.

'Right, as if you'd know!'

chapter twenty-seven

I've never been a particularly light sleeper. Even as a small kid, Mum always used to say that the house could fall down around me and they'd find me in the rubble, still in my bed, snoozing away, little zeds floating above my head. Mum was just the same too. We both love our beds.

Maybe it's because of everything that has happened recently, but I'm not falling into my usual coma these days. Tonight, I was having some stupid dream and I just woke up. It wasn't exactly a nightmare, but there was this big slavering dog that was coming towards me as I was making my way to school, and he was making this funny snivelling noise. It was punctuated by a bout of gaspy wheezing, then there'd be a big deep breath, and more snivelling and that's when I woke up. Though I'm awake, and the dream has popped, just like a bubble, I suddenly realise the noise hasn't stopped. It's real, and in my dopey state I finally work out that it's coming from Jesse's room. I lie there listening to it for a bit – it kind of starts and stops, and there's a sniffy bit in the middle – and it slowly dawns on me. It's Jesse crying.

Jesse and I had a fairly uneventful evening in the end. I had a bit of Spanish homework to finish, he was flicking through his football magazines in front of the telly. I think I was half expecting Dad to call like he said he would, but I should have known better I suppose, because he didn't. He did call the week after the funeral, as predicted, and we had some really awkward conversation. He asked all the usual adult I'm-not-really-interested-but–I-have-to-ask-type questions about homework and – it makes me cringe just to think about it – money. I told him to talk to Stu about that. Anyway, I passed the phone to Jesse, and he twittered on about his fitness training with Freya and what she had done for him and how his stamina levels had gone through the roof and then he put the phone down.

'What did he say?' I said.

'He said he'd phone again next week.'

'When?'

'Next week. He didn't say when.'

Well, this is next week and he hasn't phoned yet and maybe he won't so normal service has been resumed, I'd say.

I think Jesse also thought Dad might ring that evening, but he seemed his normal chirpy self when I reminded him at a quarter to ten that he was late for bed already according to Stu's instructions, and he shrugged his shoulders and took himself off.

So, when the crying doesn't stop, I figure I'd better go and investigate. I push back the duvet, take a quick peak at my alarm (2.05 a.m., thanks, Jesse) and creep along the landing past Uncle Stu's room (door half open, so he's not back yet) and towards his bedroom without turning on any lights. I creak open Jesse's door. It's totally dark in there, but I can hear he's definitely crying.

'Who's that?' he says through tears. I hear him sitting up in bed, but I still can't make him out clearly.

'Who do you think it is?' I say. 'The Easter bunny?' Sometimes he can be so thick, Jesse.

'Oh, it's you. Get lost,' he says.

I can hear him lying down again and I know he's pulling the duvet up to his chin like he always does. We used to share a room when we were little until the fighting got really bad and we had to be separated. I move across to his bed and perch myself on the end.

'Stu's not here, he's not back yet. What's up with you?' I whisper. 'What are you crying about?'

'What do you think I'm crying about?' he splutters. 'I couldn't sleep because I kept thinking about the finals.'

Football. I might have guessed.

'And then I got to thinking that Mum won't be there to see me play. That's if I get selected.'

He starts crying again. Only it's a bit more like sobbing this time.

'Don't be stupid,' I tell him. 'Of course you'll get selected.'

'How do you know?' says Jesse.

'Look,' I tell him, sitting forward, 'trust me. You've been playing really well this season. You set up that first goal in the quarters. You played a blinder. They're hardly going to drop you for the finals, are they?'

'Duane Mulholland is older than me, though. And after the semis, I reckon they'll go for him.'

'No chance,' I tell him. 'You may be the youngest but you're dead fast. And all that training you've been doing. Freya says she reckons you've got the edge.'

'Does she?' he sniffs. I can make him out in the dark now, and he's sitting up again.

'Course,' I say. 'Besides, they're not going to want to change a winning formula now, are they? Not when it's the finals.' I'm tempted to point out that they're hardly going to drop him when his mum's just died, but that seems unnecessarily callous.

'What about Duane Mulholland?'

'Duane Mulholland?' I practically spit the name. 'What about him? He's rubbish. He can't head a ball to save his life, and he runs like something out of *Charlie's Angels*. They're not going to pick him. Not over you.'

I haven't a clue how Duane Mulholland runs, but we watched *Charlie's Angels* on DVD recently and it was pants. When the Angels run, you could almost hear the criminals start laughing. I've also heard Jesse whine on about Duane Mulholland enough to make this sound convincing. And at two o'clock in the morning, it seems to be doing the trick. He lies back down.

'Hmm, maybe,' he says, yawning. 'I thought he was quite useful in midfield.'

'Nah,' I tell him like I'm some kind of seasoned footie pundit. 'He's rubbish. He couldn't mark his man if you gave him a great big fluorescent felt-tip pen.'

Jesse gives a little snort of laughter. Good sign, I'm thinking. Tears have stopped.

'Look,' I tell him. 'Mum may not be there, but I will be. And Uncle Stu, and Polly said she wants to come too. Freya and Jack keep asking me about it. Mind you, I can't guarantee Jack won't bring his grandad's rattle. He's convinced it brings good luck.'

'Yeah, and I'll have my lucky troll and Mum'll be watching anyway, won't she?' says Jesse as he snuggles up into the foetal position, which is how he sleeps and a sure sign he's nodding off again.

'I don't know,' I say. 'Can they get Sky Sports in heaven?'

'Very funny,' says Jesse. 'He does run a bit like Drew Barrymore, doesn't he?'

As I head back to my room, I clock Stu's open door again, and I think, why I am creeping about like this at two in the morning when he's not even here? Before I've had time to start fretting about where he might be and thinking I never had to worry about Mum off gallivanting in the middle of the night, I hear the door to the living room opening downstairs. Peeking through the gap in between the banisters, I see Stu standing in the doorway to the living room and he's talking to someone in the room, with his back to me. There's some music on low in the background – I can't quite make out what it is, just the gentle pulse of a beat – and I can't see much anyway because the light in the hall's turned off. So Jesse was right, I'm thinking. He's gone out and he's pulled. And he's brought her home.

I'm curious now, and, even though I know I'm spying, I'm rooted to the spot. He's putting his arm across the doorway in that way that blokes do when they're chatting girls up, and he's leaning in slightly and whispering something to her, and then I see a hand come round Stu's head pulling him in for a kiss. And as they kiss, they take a step out from the living room and spill over into the hall. In the murky half-light, I can see who it is he's kissing, and I put my hand over my mouth to stop a little gasp escaping because I know who the other person is. It's Luiz.

They break away from each other and take a step towards the front door. Stu opens the door and I hear him whisper, 'I'll phone you tomorrow', and then he closes the door and starts to turn, and quickly I duck my head down. He heads back into the living room to turn off the music and the lights, and I nip back into my bedroom sharpish and swiftly get into bed and pull the duvet up to my chin. My heart's beating really fast like I've been on some secret teen spy mission, and I'm trying to work out what I've just seen, and I'm wondering why is everything so *complicated* these days.

chapter twenty-eight

'You're just being naïve,' says Freya. 'Honestly, Luke, did it never cross your mind that your uncle might be gay?'

Jack, Freya and I are lolling about on the field and it's the last period before lunch on a Friday so it's mixed cricket. This is our head of sport, Mr Berry's, brilliant plan to inspire us all to play more team sports this summer – by getting boys and girls to play cricket together. As if. The good thing about this is that, if your side is in to bat and you put your names at the bottom of the list like ours, it's highly unlikely you're going to get a turn. Which suits us fine. It means I can bring my best mates up to date with what's happening on Planet Luke while the rest of the class gets on with knocking the hell out of a piece of red leather with a big block of wood.

'No, it never crossed my mind,' I say. 'Why should it? What's so naïve about that?'

I'm looking at Jack now, and he shrugs his shoulders.

'It never occurred to me,' he says, innocently.

Freya laughs.

'Never occurred to you? You haven't turned up to a PSHE lesson for the past six months! Why would it?'

'Meaning?' says Jack, snappily. Although her last sentence was whispered, he's glaring at her angrily.

'Meaning,' says Freya, on the counter-attack now, 'that when it comes to sexual matters, you're not the most enlightened of pupils at Joan of Arc, are you?'

This is the first time that any of us has made a direct reference to Jack's boycotting of sex education classes. I'm thinking, whoops, that's the cat well and truly out of the bag now, and it's off scarpering down the street.

'I'm sorry,' says Jack. 'Just because I've skived off a few PSHE classes this year doesn't make me some kind of nookie no-brainer . . .'

'Erm, excuse me,' I interject, 'I was looking for some moral support and advice from my bessie mates here about the latest bombshell in my life. I don't need another world war.'

Freya and Jack look at me and sigh. There's a brief ripple of applause. Heidi Lundquist, who would win the strongest girl in the school competition hands down, has just smacked the cricket ball across the boundary and towards the school kitchen for six. With a little more effort, it might have ended up in the custard. Ted Maher shouts, 'You go, Heidi!' He's always had a thing about her, though she towers over him and so obviously isn't interested.

'Moral support?' says Freya, ignoring Heidi's prowess. 'What moral support do you need? Just because you've got a gay uncle – it's his life, for God's sake. What's it got to do with you?'

'He's my guardian now,' I remind her, 'in case you hadn't noticed. He's the one who's looking after me.'

'Well, so what?' says Freya. 'Does it really make any difference to you if he dates men or women? He's an adult. Just because he's taken over the role of dad in your life doesn't mean he can't have a life of his own.'

'A private life, even,' says Jack.

'Private life?' What are you getting at now?'

'Well, if he hasn't told you he's gay,' he continues, 'I'd say that's because he doesn't want you to know.'

Heidi clouts another ball over towards the science block this time, and the rest of the class bursts into spontaneous cheering. We clap madly too, Freya shouts, 'Bravo, Heidi!' at the top of her voice, knowing the longer her innings continues, the less likely it becomes we'll be called upon to show off our batting skills. Or lack of them.

'Probably because it's none of your business,' says Freya, examining her split ends up close and trying to tear them apart with her fingernails.

'He's not taking over the role of "dad" in my life anyway,' I point out. 'I have a dad. You saw him, remember?'

Freya raises her eyebrows in mock surprise as if to say, 'You've changed your tune.'

'Oh, and how many times has your darling dad called since the funeral?' says Freya. She starts counting up on her fingers, gets to ten and then counts back down again. 'I'd make that once. Not exactly ringing the phone off the hook, is he? Look, Luke, your uncle's a lovely bloke who's given everything up to look after you and your brother. Just because he prefers men to women doesn't mean he'll be any better or worse at it. Give him a break.'

'He might be better,' Jack says. 'There's loads of same sex couples adopting kids these days. The papers are full of them. Look at that kid in 8T. He's got two mums. Lesbians. He seems all right.'

'I never said he wasn't great,' I object, ignoring Jack and his lesbians. 'I just wish he'd told me. I felt so . . . so . . .'

'Left out?' says Freya. 'You felt stupid because he kept something from you. Look, welcome to the real world, Luke. You've only ever had your mum – and she treated you more like a partner than a kid. She told you everything. But parents aren't always like that. My mum and dad are fairly open, admittedly, but I know kids whose parents hardly speak to them, let alone discuss their private life.'

'I only found out last week that my parents are going to the Maldives this summer,' says Jack, looking affronted. 'Without me. They never even asked me.'

'What I think,' says Freya, 'is, if you're worried, you ought to talk to him about it. Tell him what you saw. It's no good pussyfooting around.'

'Yeah,' I say. They're right, I know they are. Annoyingly, Freya's always right. Except when it comes to science. Never copy her science homework. She's crap at science.

'The Maldives?' says Freya impressed. 'Did they win the lottery? It's not cheap. I've seen the pictures, though. It looks like some tropical paradise.'

'Wouldn't know,' says Jack. 'I'll show you the postcard – if they bother to send me one.'

'So, what are you meant to do while your parents are swanking off to the Maldives?' I ask. I'm thinking, there's me being a selfish git, worrying about my problems, when all the time my mates have got problems of their own.

'Oh, they've very thoughtfully organised for me to go and stay at my gran's.'

'I thought she was dead,' says Freya, screwing her eyes up against the sun.

'Not her. That was my nan. No, my other gran,' says Jack.

'Not the one who lives . . .' I begin.

Jack sighs loudly.

'Yes, the one who lives in Inverness.'

Freya and I look at each other and try not to laugh.

'It's the wrong time of the year to go to the Maldives,' she points out. 'You'll be much better off in Scotland.'

'With a retired PE teacher?' asks Jack. 'Her idea of a fun time is a five-mile jog followed by a cold shower and porridge. With lumps.'

'Och, grim,' says Freya in a surprisingly good Scottish accent.

'Well, at least you won't have to worry about getting sunburnt,' I point out.

Heidi whacks another ball straight at the bowler, Andrew Shelby, who instinctively holds up his arm and catches her out in an incredible display of hand/eye coordination.

'Howzat!' shouts someone.

'Do you know, until this term, I never knew people actually said that?' says Freya. 'It's quaint, isn't it?'

Mr Berry's arm shoots up.

'Out!'

'Do you think we'll ever actually have to bat this term?' says Jack as Ethan Todd strides up to the crease.

'No, not today, anyway,' says Freya, brightly. 'Look there's only fifteen minutes to lunch now.' She holds up her watch triumphantly. She wears this big old bloke's watch from the Seventies that she bought in a jumble sale a few years ago. It's all shiny chrome – 'a design classic', she calls it. 'So it's the final, on Saturday? Jesse's getting all keyed up about that. He's training really hard. You coming, Jack?'

'This Saturday?' He's sucking on a blade of grass. 'Yeah, why not?'

'You'll be there?' she says to me.

'Of course I'll be there,' I say. 'I don't have much choice.'

'You'll love it really,' Freya enthuses. 'They're expecting a big crowd, Jesse says. And I know exactly what I'm going to wear . . .'

At the end of history, our last lesson of the day, I'm ready to make a quick getaway. I shove my books in my bag and make a dash for the library. I just need somewhere quiet to think things through, and I know on a Friday it'll be deserted. I won't be disturbed in here. There are two studious Year Eights doing their homework, and the school librarian, Mrs Curren, is looking at something on screen as I go in, and gives me a smile as I take a seat in the far corner by the non-fiction. It's normally dead at this time of day and I figure that's just what I need to sort my head out.

I'm running through stuff in my own mind, trying to work it out – what I saw, what it means, what I'll say to Stu – when I look up and I see Mrs Curren watching me out of the corner of her eye. I fish out some homework from my bag just to make it look more convincing.

I like her, Mrs Curren. I remember when I was in Year Seven we were told we had to bring a book in for private reading every week. Some kids already had books, but a few of us didn't, so I went along to the library. We stood around, about five of us, looking gormless and acting like we knew what we were doing. She took it in turns to have a chat with us all, get to know our names, ask us what we were interested in. Then she sat us down at the big table in the middle and brought a pile of books along. We all looked at the covers and chatted a bit, and bit by bit, we'd pick up a book that she'd talked about and I could see she was match-making us. She pushed a book called *Holes* in my direction, and told me a little bit about it – not too much, so I wouldn't need to read it, but just enough to get the interest levels up. I got so into it that I read it in a couple of days.

'Gosh, that was quick,' she said when I brought it back. 'What do you fancy next?'

I look up now, and there she is, standing right in front of me. She's wearing blue jeans and a green cardigan, with a row of pearls, and she's got a very snazzy bob. Very elegant, Mrs Curren. Bit of classic, bit of modern.

'Not reading today, Luke?' she asks in her sing-song voice. I always thought libraries were places that were meant to be pin-drop quiet, with heels squeaking on the polished flooring, but Mrs Curren says, 'Speak up, it's a library not a cemetery' when people start whispering at her. She told me once that she was a bit deaf, and she couldn't hear when people whispered, but I think that's just a pretence. 'I like to keep a lively library,' she says.

'No, Mrs Curren. Just some homework.'

'I was sorry to hear the news about your mother, Luke.' She puts her hand on my shoulder. 'How are things at home?'

'Oh, it's okay,' I tell her. 'My uncle lives with us now.'

I'm thinking I could do without this, but she sits down next to me and I can hardly tell her to bog off (which I wouldn't do anyway, because I like her).

'How's that going? You and your brother getting on okay with him?'

'Yeah,' I say truthfully. 'I think so. It's different. He's never had kids before so I suppose it takes a bit of getting used to. And he's moved down from Manchester to look after us.'

'Manchester?' she says. 'That's quite a change of scenery for your uncle. He must care very much about you and your brother to uproot himself like that.'

'Yes,' I say, realising I've never thought about this before. 'Yes, I think he does.'

'You've had a lot of upheaval in your lives recently,' says Mrs Curren. 'But it's good to hear you're sorting yourselves out.' She looks straight at me, as though she can see exactly what's going on in my head. How does she do that?

'It's early days, Luke,' says Mrs Curren. 'Getting to know each other takes time. These things always do, you know. As long as you keep talking, you'll find a way through.' She stands up and starts moving back towards her desk. 'And don't neglect your reading, either,' she throws over her shoulder. 'Books can make sense of all sorts of things life chucks at us, believe me. I'd never have got through my divorce without Marian Keyes.'

chapter twenty-nine

I slam the front door behind me with my usual vigour, yell 'I'm back!' and dump my bag in the hall. In my head I can hear some kind of echo, Mum barking 'Don't leave that there!', so I pick it up off the carpet where I'd left it and lug it up to my bedroom. When I come back down, Stu calls out, 'I'm in the kitchen' and I find him chopping vegetables.

'Jesse at football practice again?' he asks.

'Yes,' I say, shoving two slices of bread into the toaster. 'He's bricking it. They announce the final squad for tomorrow at training this afternoon.'

Stu nods.

'That's going to be one very disappointed kid if he doesn't get picked for the big match,' he says. He's laying into a green pepper as though he has a personal grudge against it. 'Don't fill yourself up on toast,' he warns. 'I'm doing a stir-fry.'

'Don't worry, I'll eat that, too,' I reassure him. 'I'm a growing teenager, remember?'

'Yes, you start chewing furniture if you haven't eaten anything for more than five minutes,' he says.

'Tea?' I hold up the kettle and he nods.

'Yeah, why not?'

There's a little pause here while I fill it up – and while I'm plucking up the courage to say *something*, he nips in there first.

'Luke,' he begins, 'I'm glad Jesse's not here. I wanted to have a quiet word.'

Oh-oh, this sounds ominous. 'Quiet word' in my experience means a no-nonsense, stop-beating-around-the-bush bollocking. I can practically see the storm clouds gathering on the horizon, and my pulse starts racing. I concentrate very hard on buttering two slices of wholemeal toast.

'Last night,' he carries on, speaking quite slowly and deliberately as though he's being very picky in his choice of words, 'I got a lift home from a friend who came in for a drink.'

I throw a couple of teabags in two mugs as nonchalantly as I can manage and start pouring on boiling water.

'And when my friend left, I think you were still up, weren't you?' He's still chopping, but I figure it's just so he doesn't have to look me in the eye. His knife motion isn't quite so energetic now.

'I wasn't still up,' I explain, putting my toast down on the plate. 'I had gone to bed when you told me to. But it's just that Jesse got a bit upset, so I went to see what was wrong with him.'

'But you were watching from upstairs, weren't you?'

'No . . . well, yes. I mean, I wasn't spying . . .'

'But you did see me saying goodbye to my friend?' says Stu.

'Yes, I saw you saying goodbye to Luiz.' I figure it's time for one of us to come clean.

'Ah, right,' he says, looking a bit sheepish. 'I thought I saw something moving on the landing out of the corner of my eye.' He stops chopping and puts down the knife as I pass him his tea.

'Are you angry?' I ask.

'No, not with you.' He shakes his head in a resigned way. 'Only with myself.'

There's a pause. I know I have to say something.

'It's not a crime to be gay, you know. Why didn't you tell us?'

Stu takes a deep breath. 'Oh, it wasn't that I hadn't thought about it. I had. But you and Jesse both had so much to contend with, what with Patty and her illness. The last thing I wanted to do was drag you through another emotional minefield.'

He motions to the kitchen table, the veg chopping

abandoned for the time being, and we both sit down with our tea and what's left of my toast.

'But why did you keep it secret? You could have just told me, you know.'

'It wasn't meant to be a secret,' he protests. 'I'm not ashamed about being gay. It's hard to explain really. I'd never wanted to hide it, but I'd never found the right time to tell you. I know it was a cop-out, but I suppose I was afraid how you might react.'

'Did Mum know?' I ask.

'Yes, of course,' he gives a little wry smile. 'She's always known. She used to joke that she knew before I did! I don't know why she never mentioned it. Once a Catholic, I suppose. And then she had so many other things to worry about – her illness, what the consequences might be, what the future would be like for you two if she died. Me being gay wasn't really top of her agenda.'

'You mean it didn't really matter?' I ask him.

'I suppose so. It never bothered her so I suppose she didn't think it was an issue.' He stops and takes a sip of his tea.

'It's not,' I say.

'Not what?'

'An issue,' I tell him. 'It doesn't matter. Why should it? What happened to Mum has mucked your life up as much as ours – more in fact. Jesse and I are still at the same school, with the same friends, living in the same house, thanks to you. You're the one who's given everything up for us.'

Stu puts his hand on my shoulder and gives it a little pat. Without wishing to sound like a total dishcloth (wet and very sloppy), he's given me a few hugs since Mum died, and I can't deny it's helped. I reckon now is as good a time as any for me to return the favour. I can see he's a bit choked up – his eyes look glassy and he's quiet for a moment afterwards and then he takes a big gulp of tea.

'Look,' he says softly, 'I didn't *have* to do this, look after you two. It's my choice. It's what I want, to be here with you and Jesse. We're family, and that's what families do – they help each other. They depend on each other. And you know what? I wouldn't have it any other way. I'd reached a point in my life where I needed a new start. I even needed some responsibility. There was stuff that was wrong in my life, that I needed to change, and I'm sorting that now. But what I can't change is what I am, who I am.'

'You don't have to change, that's what I'm saying,' I tell him. 'I don't want you to change and I bet Jesse doesn't either.'

He looks at me and raises his eyebrows. 'Really?' He picks up a piece of my toast and steals a crafty bite.

'Yeah, really. Except maybe those trainers.'

Stu looks down at his feet. He's wearing these dodgy all-white trainers that are totally spotless and horribly naff. They look as though he's just sauntered straight out of Nasty Trainers R Us.

'What?' he says. 'What's wrong with them?'

'What's right with them?' I tell him. 'Next time you go trainer shopping, I'd better come along too.'

'What are you, the fashion police?' He laughs and goes back to chopping his vegetables.

'I'm only being honest,' I say. 'It's the best policy, you know.'

'Yeah, yeah, I think I got the message,' says Stu. 'By the way, you didn't mention anything to Jesse about . . . about last night and Luiz did you?'

'No,' I tell him truthfully. 'I avoid Jesse like the plague at school – it's bad enough seeing him at home every day.'

'Well, make yourself scarce after supper and I'll tell him tonight,' he says. 'No point in hanging about, is there?'

'Not wearing those trainers, no,' I say, and race out of the kitchen as he hurls a rather large carrot at my head.

When Jesse gets home, it's good news. He stands on the doorstep ringing the bell and screaming through the letterbox, 'I'm in! I'm in!' like some kind of demented postman, so we somehow manage to work out that Jesse has indeed been selected to play for Joan of Arc comprehensive in the Inter-County Schools Under-16s Challenge Final tomorrow. Stu and I are in a good mood too. We've cleared the air now and it feels better, and I never thought I'd admit it but I'm getting excited at the prospect of the big match. Once we've wolfed down the chicken stir-fry (we like), I start getting up from the table.

'It's your turn to do the washing up, Luke,' says Jesse.

Before I can tell him where to stick his rubber gloves, Stu says, 'No, I'm on washing-up duty tonight, Jesse, and you're going to help me. I want the full lowdown on tomorrow's match. Now, what are Thurston like in midfield . . .?'

So while Stu starts buttering up Jesse for his heart-to-heart, I nip off upstairs to phone Freya and admit that, as usual, she's right and I was wrong. The thing about Freya is, she's not one of those 'told you so' merchants. After I relate the afternoon's conversation, she says, 'I'm really proud of you, Luke,' and that makes me feel even better because Freya never says stuff she doesn't mean.

'How's Jesse taking it?' she asks.

'Doesn't know yet. Well, at least he might do by now. Stu's telling him, while they wash up.'

'Ooh, the night before the big match,' she says. 'It's not going to upset him, is it?'

'Ah, I never thought of that,' I admit, 'and I don't think Stu did either. Well, he must have told him by now. I'd better go and find out how it's gone down. What time are we meeting tomorrow?'

'I'll be there fifteen minutes before the match,' says Freya.

'You don't want to come round here first? We can give you a lift.'

'No, I've got some finishing touches to put to my outfit,' she says. 'I'm having a few problems with the chicken wire.'

When I get downstairs, Jesse is lolling all over the sofa watching more football on the box. No sign of Stu, but as I look out through the window, I can see he's in the garden on his mobile to someone.

'Feet,' I say as I go to sit down, and Jesse grudgingly gives up half the sofa space to me.

'Help Stu with the washing up, did you?' I ask.

Jesse is totally engrossed by the game.

'What? Oh yeah,' he says. Totally vacant, as usual.

'Did you have a little chat?'

He looks at me, puzzled. 'Chat?'

'You know – did he say anything to you?'

He bottled it, I'm thinking. Stu didn't have the guts to tell him after all.

'What, you mean that's he's gay?' says Jesse, still

riveted to all the little players bombing around the pitch after the ball.

'Oh. He did tell you then?'

Jesse throws me another perplexed look.

'Yeah.' He turns his head back to the TV. 'I don't mind,' says Jesse, picking up the remote and bumping up the volume a couple of notches. 'Why, does it bother you?'

'Me – no,' I tell him. 'I don't know why he didn't tell us before. Bit silly keeping it quiet. Sometimes I wonder about Mum, you know.'

'What? She wasn't gay was she?' says Jesse, his mouth dropping open.

'No, you prat. I mean, she never mentioned boyfriends, did she? Dad ran off and got a new life with a new wife and kids, but Mum never had anyone else after Dad.'

'As far as we know,' says Jesse. 'But I don't think she did. She would have said.'

'I suppose we took up all her time. Well, us and work. I wish she had had boyfriends,' I say. 'I wish she'd had more fun while she was alive.'

'Stu's got a boyfriend,' says Jesse, smirking. 'He told me. And I know who it is!'

'Yes, so do I,' I say. 'It's Luiz, isn't it? The nurse from the hospital.'

'Oh, you knew,' he says slightly disappointed. 'Ah,

but I bet you didn't know that he might be coming tomorrow.'

'Tomorrow?' I say. 'Where? Here?'

'You know Luiz is from Brazil and he always used to talk to me about the footie because he's such a big fan too? Well, Stu's going to ask him if he wants to come to the match tomorrow.'

Right on cue, Stu bursts into the room, waving the phone.

'Looks like you've got a big, bald, noisy Brazilian to cheer Joan of Arc along. Luiz is on lates tomorrow so he can come to the match.'

He looks at me and asks, 'You don't mind, do you?'

'No,' I smile back. 'I like Luiz. And anyway, Jesse and his mates are going to need all the support they can get.'

chapter thirty

It's not just an army that marches on its stomach, says Stu. He reckons a team plays on it too, so on Saturday morning he's up bright and early, armed with his trusty wok, and he's frying bacon, sausages, mushrooms and anything else he can find in the fridge that's not past its sell-by date, including an aubergine. The smell of sizzling bacon is better than any alarm clock and, even though Jesse claims he's not hungry and can't even *begin* to think about food, he sits down anyway and we all get stuck in to the kind of breakfast that Mum called 'a heart attack on a plate' and reserved solely for Christmases, birthdays and other special occasions.

'This *is* a special occasion,' Stu replies, when I point this out. 'Not every day is it that my nephew gets through to the Inter-State . . . erm, what is it again, Jesse?'

'Inter-County Schools Under-16s Challenge Final.' Jesse rattles it off as though it's some kind of tongue-twister he's been practising for the past five years (which, in a way, it is).

'Exactly,' says Stu. 'Anyway, you'll need all your strength to lift that cup this afternoon.' He raises his own mug, raises it to toast Jesse and his team's success, and takes a big swig of tea.

'It's not a cup,' says Jesse, who seems to be managing to force down fried egg and sausage quite happily despite his initial protests. 'It's actually a big silver plate.'

'Oh, is it?' says Stu, feigning disappointment. 'What a shame. Maybe I won't go after all . . .'

Jesse looks up at him for a moment and I swear he falls for this.

'Jesse,' I say, 'did you hear they've taken the word "gullible" out of the English dictionary?'

'Have they?' he answers, right on cue.

'Don't tease your brother on his big day,' says Stu wagging his knife at me playfully. 'He needs to think positive thoughts and concentrate on the game ahead. That's what Sir Alf Ramsey would say.'

Jesse and I look at each other.

'Who?'

Stu rolls his eyes. 'Just get on with your breakfast.'

Ten minutes later, there's a panic.

'Is my kit clean?' Jesse stands up so suddenly he manages to knock his chair over.

Stu puts a friendly hand on his shoulder. 'Relax,' he says. 'You'll be a nervous wreck by midday. It's washed and neatly folded and it's in your sports bag along with all the rest of your stuff and your lucky troll. Now sit down and finish your breakfast or you're not going anywhere.'

Amazingly, Jesse picks up the chair and does exactly what he's told. He must be more nervous than I thought.

'Right, it's kick off at twelve-thirty, so I'm going to take you down to the sports ground for twelve. That gives us time to nab the best seats,' says Stu, looking at me.

'What about Luiz?' I ask. 'Isn't he coming?'

'Yes,' says Stu, carrying the dirty plates over to the sink. 'He's meeting us there, though. He lives over on the Nuffield Estate so he'll make his own way. What about your mates, Luke? They coming here first?'

'No,' I tell him. 'They'll meet us there.'

'Right,' he says. 'Luke, you're washing up, I'm tidying up, and Jesse, you can get into your tracky bottoms and get outside for a bit of a warm up, yeah? Thunderbirds are go!'

By eleven-thirty, Jesse is going through his kit bag for the umpteenth time, checking that everything's in order: boots, shirt, shorts, socks, hair gel, lucky troll –

all the essentials for the modern footballer. Stu comes down the stairs and he's wearing a pair of jeans, a blue T-shirt and some hippy sandals that are a minor improvement on yesterday's trainers. Jesse looks up and his mouth falls open.

'Blue,' he stammers, as if in shock. 'That's Thurston Academy team colours . . .'

'Oh,' says Stu, looking at me. 'I didn't realise you took it all that seriously.' I point triumphantly to the red Joan of Arc polo shirt I've put on – it's actually part of my PE kit, but I figured I ought to show willing – and Stu nods and goes back upstairs. He's gone for ages and Jesse starts to pick his nose nervously as though his life depends on seeking out every trace of bogey, so I nip upstairs to find out what's holding him up. I open the door to his room, and Stu is foraging through a pile of clothes on the bed like a maniac.

'It's a footie match, not a fashion show,' I tell him. 'A red T-shirt will do.'

'I haven't got anything red,' he says, looking desperate. 'It's not my colour.'

'It is today,' I tell him. 'Look, there's a red top. Put that on.'

'That's a pyjama jacket,' he says. 'I can't wear that.'

'We don't have time for all this,' I say, thinking I'm the one who sounds like a parent. 'Just put it on and get in the car.'

He puts on the red pyjama jacket with cream piping and goes downstairs.

'Ta-da,' he says to Jesse. 'Look – red.'

'Can we go now?' says Jesse, looking up. 'I'm feeling a bit sick.'

'Don't worry,' says Stu as he opens the front door to usher us out. 'It's only nerves – it's all the adrenalin. I always felt sick before a big school match.'

'I didn't know you played football for your school?' says Jesse.

'I didn't,' says Stu as he shoves Jesse's kit in the boot. 'It was chess. I played chess for the school.'

I try and choke down a giggle, but it turns into a sort of grunt.

'Did you ever win?' I ask, trying to cover it up and not laugh. Even Jesse is starting to smirk.

'No,' he says, starting up the car. 'We were rubbish.'

Halfway to the sports ground, Jesse shouts, 'Stop the car!' Stu screeches to a halt, Jesse flings open his door, narrowly missing a lamppost, and proceeds to empty the contents of his stomach – Uncle Stu's half-digested cholesterol-fest – into the gutter. I'm sitting up front next to Stu so I pass Jesse back some tissues from the glove compartment.

'Better now?' I ask, as Stu pulls off again, leaving Jesse's pavement pizza behind.

'Yes, a bit,' he says. 'Sorry. It just all came up. I think it was that aubergine . . .'

'Hold on,' says Stu, 'we'll be there in just a few minutes.'

As Stuart's Golf pulls into the car park, Luiz is just reversing into a space opposite in a beat-up old rust-bucket of a Volvo.

'How's my star player today?' he shouts across as Jesse gets out of the car.

'All right,' says Jesse. 'Bit nervous. I'd better go . . .' and he points towards the changing room before dashing off to join his team-mates.

'I didn't know you were a big football fan, Luke,' says Luiz, looking at me.

'I'm not,' I say. 'It's a bit of moral support, you know.'

Stu is just getting out of the car and comes round to greet Luiz. They hug – nothing sloppy, no kissing or anything – and then Luiz turns to me.

'I brought some things to make the noise,' he says, holding up a backpack with an evil glint in his eye. 'In Brazil, we like the matches to have lots of noise.'

'I'm not sure how well that'll go down round here,' I tell him as we take our place on the terraces. I send Jack a reminder text just in case he's got any ideas about wheedling his way out of this match.

'Where are you?' I text him and he texts back, 'On

229

my way, José'. I send the same message to Freya and she messages me back saying, 'Right behind you!' and when I turn round, yup, there she is.

Freya has painted her face in red-and-white stripes and is wearing the biggest, most ridiculous hat I've ever seen. It's about a metre tall, red-and-white striped, and is emblazoned with our school crest and motto 'Through valour, sweet victory'. She's also got a red bolero jacket, red-and-white striped feather boa, the baggiest white pants I've ever seen, and some red platform shoes that raise her up about fifteen centimetres. Whoever stands behind her is going to get a seriously restricted view of the match.

'Do you like it?' she says as she comes tottering down the terraces, concentrating hard on not falling off her wedge heels.

'Sorry, I didn't realise the ticket stated fancy dress,' I say.

'Honestly, Luke, stop being so suburban. It's football! It's the final! Loosen up, enjoy!' cries Freya as she starts shimmying back and forth. 'I made it all myself,' she says proudly, twirling around to give us a better view. 'You can't believe how difficult it was to shape the chicken wire properly. That stuff's got a mind of its own.'

'You look fabulous,' says Luiz. 'It's like the Mardi Gras has come to Portshead.'

'Oh, do you think so?' cries Freya, delighted, holding the hat on with one hand. 'Hello, Stu, and you must be Luiz. Pleased to meet you.' She holds out her hand and Luiz kisses it. This causes Freya to whoop with delight and start dancing again. Luiz eggs her on by clapping his hands together, and singing what can only be some kind of wild Brazilian chant. Other supporters are starting to fill up the stand now and, although there are a few scarves, no one seems to have gone to Freya's lengths and our little party is attracting a bit of attention.

'Afternoon, everybody,' says Jack.

I'm pleased to see he's not wearing a silly hat but he has got the notorious parka on, and he's got the hood up.

'Bit overdressed for a day like today, aren't you, Jack?' says Stu.

'Oh, I only wore this to get here,' says Jack and he removes the coat to reveal a red-and-white striped football shirt and matching red-and-white hair.

'It's my grandad's Sunderland shirt, but it is red and white. And my mum did the hair for me this morning,' he says, sheepishly. 'What do you think?'

'You've all gone stark raving mad,' I say.

'It was Freya's idea. I've brought the can with me too if you want to do yours,' he adds hopefully, holding up the red hair paint. 'I left the white at home though. There wasn't much left.'

'Come on, Luke,' says Stu, 'It's only ten minutes to kick off. Let's put a bit of colour on these terraces.'

He grabs the can off Jack, and tosses it to Luiz who starts spraying Stu's hair. I suddenly get a flashback to that last weekend with Mum, rolling around laughing as we tried on all those ridiculous wigs in stupid colours that Mia and Polly had brought home for her.

Luiz passes the canister to Freya when he's finished and she starts towards me with a manic glint in her eye.

'Your turn, Luke,' she announces, shaking the can as she speaks.

Jack jabs me in the ribs with his elbow and whispers, 'What is your uncle wearing? It looks like his pyjamas . . .'

'Oh, it's a long story,' I say as I shut my eyes and Freya starts squirting red paint in my direction.

chapter thirty-one

As the two teams troop out on to the pitch, it seems to be the general signal for the supporters to start behaving like a bunch of soccer-crazed hooligans. Luiz has produced a small set of bongos from his backpack and starts to bash away like a pro, making a not inconsiderable amount of noise that echoes around the sports ground. Not only does it get the Joan of Arc fans going, but the rivals also seem to be enjoying the crazy *thud thud thud* of the Brazilian rhythms. The place is filling up now and there must be a few hundred spectators – though it could just as well be the World Cup final as far as we're all concerned. Luiz has also brought along one of those extremely loud aerosol hooters that he's handed over to Freya (very unwisely, I'd say). She gives it a good blast straight off and practically blows half the supporters off the terraces.

'Well, that seems to be working quite well,' she says.

Jack has the secret weapon of course, his grandad's rattle, that hasn't yet made an appearance, although he says he's saving it for our first goal, ban or no ban, which seems a bit over-confident for a born pessimist like Jack.

Mia has turned up with her husband Andy and their two kids and they've joined our party now, and Polly arrives five minutes into the match, showering us all with kisses and – almost literally – fizzy wine. She's also brought along homemade lemonade for us non-drinkers, so sharp it makes your teeth itch. Once the drinks have been distributed, she proudly unfurls a huge banner with Mia that reads 'BURN 'EM UP, JOAN OF ARC!'

'You don't think it's in bad taste, do you?' she asks as Mia takes a slug of her wine.

'Just because you're a Christian martyr doesn't mean you can't have a sense of humour,' Mia responds, tucking into the industrial-sized quantities of sandwiches she's made for everyone. She and Polly have become good mates now, and they often meet up at work. Sometimes they come round together to see the three of us too.

'You know, it's funny how we hated each other at first,' says Polly, hanging on to Mia's arm. 'You thought I was trying to muscle in on your friendship with Pat, and I thought you were a possessive old cow. Silly to think that that's what brought us together.'

'Well, that and the wigs,' says Mia, pouring wine.

The teams are led out on to the pitch by the managers.

In our case, it's Mr 'Rottweiler' Rubinstein, who makes Alex Ferguson look like a kindergarten teacher. He's got a dogged look on his face today, as though he wants to settle an old score, chewing gum compulsively and checking his watch. The ref is a young black guy with a goatee that's he's dyed blond and, after a bit of coin-tossing, some shaking of the hands that seems to involve everyone except the spectators, and much discussion between the ref and his two linesmen, he blows his whistle and Thurston kick off.

For the first ten minutes, there's nothing much happening. Callum, our captain, is shouting orders at his players (so's Rottweiler, naturally), trying to get them all to settle. Jesse looks as though he's recovered from his dodgy stomach and I notice Duane Mulholland is on the subs' bench, which means that Jesse's fairy godmother has come up trumps again.

'They're just getting the measure of each other,' Freya says. She's gone into her commentary-box mode, which is mainly for the benefit of Jack and me. 'There's a lot of nerves on that pitch right now, but they'll soon get down to it.'

'The other team is weak in midfield,' Luiz adds knowledgeably, and then points to the far side of the pitch. 'But watch that kid on the right wing – he's dangerous. I think he's good enough to play for Brazil one day.'

Luiz is right, of course. Their number 10 is a cool latin-looking kid with a tan face and his floppy black hair tied back by a bandana. His long legs are on the skinny side, but he must have turbo-powered boots because there's some serious acceleration when he runs and the Thurston kids start yelling for Fabrizzio.

'How's my favourite boy?' Polly sneaks up behind me and wraps her arms round me in a big hug. 'Everything fine in Lukesville? How are you getting on with Stu?'

'Yeah,' I tell her, trying hard not to blush from the very public display of affection that I'm still not quite used to. 'We're settling in. Had our ups and downs, you know. I think we've all realised that being open and honest with each other is important.'

'Ah yes.' Polly knows immediately what I'm talking about. 'I must admit, I did see that little cloud on the horizon. I tried to warn Stu, but you know, strictly speaking, that kind of thing is none of my business – I can't really get involved with the family side.'

She takes a bite of her sandwich and chews thoughtfully for a bit. 'I don't think he was being dishonest though, Luke. He thought he was protecting you and Jesse. Sometimes, you know, people can do the wrong thing with the best of intentions.'

'Did you know that Stu was gay?' I ask, turning to face her. We've moved a few metres away from the others and are well out of earshot, and I figure this is a good time for the billion dollar question. 'I always thought you had a bit of a thing for him?'

'Well, to be honest,' Polly explains, 'I did have quite a crush initially. Fortunately, I revealed all to your mum one afternoon before I had the chance of making a complete fool of myself. She told me in no uncertain terms that I was barking up the wrong tree, or sniffing round the wrong lamppost as she put it.'

She looks across at Stu and Luiz. They're having a laugh over some shared joke and look like they've been together for years.

'They'll be good together, Stu and Luiz,' she says. 'Luiz is a lovely bloke. He has that knack of making people feel relaxed whenever he's around – that's why he's such a good nurse. He was brilliant with your Mum, you know. I like to think Patty played her part in bringing the two of them together.' Polly's eyes twinkle conspiratorially, and she whispers, 'She was always talking to Luiz about her "lovely brother". I think she knew they'd make a good match.'

'Yeah, sounds like Mum,' I say.

She agrees, looking me in the eyes. 'I think she probably knew that, if Stuart was to make a success of looking after you and Jesse, he'd need some support,' says Polly. 'And I don't think you can get better than Luiz.'

Over on the field, Saul Cox, one of the mainstays of Joan of Arc's defence, is chopped down by some evil-looking kid in a number 3 shirt from Thurston and the ref blows his whistle.

'Oi, ref!' shouts Freya. 'Dirty foul!'

'Yellow card!' yells Jack, who seems to be getting the hang of shouting at the ref.

Stu swears loudly, calling into question their number 3's parentage and his personal hygiene. We've got a free kick from just outside the box. Shav's taking it – a sure sign he'll have a pot at the goal. This is one of Joan of Arc's set pieces that they've been practising – Jesse's been harping on about it most nights – and Shav can bend a ball like a boomerang, according to legend. Well, according to Jesse.

Everything goes quiet. Even Luiz quits the bongo-bashing for a moment. We all take a deep breath and build up with a huge 'WHOOOOAAAH!' as Shav starts his run-up. He strikes the ball so sweetly with the inside of his left foot and it curves up into the air in a graceful arc. It's almost as though it's been whisked away by an angel and I can see the Thurston goalie leap off his line and stretch a hand into the air, but you can see he'll never reach it. This shot is heading away from him, towards the far corner and he doesn't stand a chance. It curves beautifully and starts to drop and, just for a moment, I can't bear to look and I close my eyes. Then I hear the THUD THUD THUD of Luiz bashing away on his drums, and Freya shrieks like a banshee at the top of her voice, and when I open them again the ball is sitting in the back of the net and we all go ballistic.

CLACK-CLACK-CLACK. Jack has winched up his grandad's rattle and twirled it wildy round his head. He must have been practising with that monstrous thing because it's not light, though I've no idea where you can make a noise like that in public without having some kind of Asbo slapped on you. Everyone turns to stare and even Rottweiler Rubinstein seems to have half a smile on his face.

One-nil! Only ten minutes to half-time now, and we're one-nil up.

'Give us another, Joan of Arc!' screeches Freya, hopping around in excitement, her hat wobbling about like a lunatic tower.

The next ten minutes is fraught. Thurston know they're at a big disadvantage if they go into half-time one-nil down, but they're looking edgy now, and their passing seems to be shot to pieces. Mark Chetley has a good run on the left wing, but they've got a lad called Nish who stops him dead in his track and boots the ball back up our end. Meanwhile, Jesse seems to be making a fair job of clearing up their messy passes in midfield. When the ref blows the half-time whistle, a wave of relief sweeps over us.

'Well, I think they've earned their oranges,' says Jack.

'Never mind oranges, I think I've earned another drink,' says Polly, mopping her brow.

chapter thirty-two

'JOAN OF ARC, RULE DA PARK! JOAN OF ARC, RULE DA PARK!'

As the teams troop back on to the pitch, a spontaneous round of chanting breaks out on the other side of the stands, so Luiz picks up the beat and starts bashing along on his bongos and we all join in, Freya standing aloft on her heels, conducting everyone.

That's Thurston's cue to start some singing of their own, and they break into their school anthem which turns out to be what Jack calls a 'tuneless dirge'. If the second half is going to be as hotly contested as the titan struggle that's going on between the singing spectators, this should be worth watching. I have to admit that this is more fun than history homework which is probably what I'd be doing if I weren't here.

Rottweiler Rubinstein takes his seat on the bench with Duane Mulholland and another couple of nervy-looking kids. From the look on his face, you'd swear Rottweiler has been chewing wasps, not gum, although the Thurston coach doesn't seem a 'shiny happy people' type either. He looks like he's gone a few rounds in the boxing ring with Mike Tyson, and he's got the cauliflower ears and flattened nose to show for it. You wouldn't want to meet him on any night, let alone a dark one.

Whatever the boxer/coach said to his team during half-time seems to have done the trick, though. They have a steely determination about them now, and as soon as they kick off, you can see they're communicating better with each other, shouting out orders, and concentrating much harder. Within the first five minutes, their dangerous right winger – the crowd chant 'Fabrizzio, Fabrizzio' every time he so much as touches the ball – has made a break and taken a soft-ish pot at goal. Although it's not too testing for Ali, our keeper, they're making a statement. 'We're fighting back.' Stu and I catch each other's eyes for a moment, and I can tell exactly what he's thinking: please don't let them score.

We've never really talked about it, but I think we both know how important this match is to Jesse. It's not just about who stands there at the end of ninety minutes holding up a big shiny silver cup – sorry, plate – grinning cheesily from ear to ear. For Jesse, football has become his escape route, the valve that he uses to let off steam when it all gets too horrible. No matter how much dirty stuff hits the fan, he's still got his footie. So your dad leaves home, but as long as you can kick a ball, you're okay. Looking back, that was when Jesse's interest in football began. Then your mum gets sick, you get some evil old battleaxe to look after you, but there's still training and matches and winning to concentrate on. And when your mum eventually dies – and let's face it, life can't get much worse for an almost twelve-year-old kid at that point – there's still the final to look forward to, a reason to keep struggling on through the mire. I remember thinking what a prat Jesse was when he started talking to Dad at Mum's funeral about football and the final, but I realise now, that was the most natural thing in the world to him. This isn't just about football. It's a lifeline for Jesse. It's what's kept him going through the toughest times he's ever had to face.

So when Stu and I look across at each other, we can see a flash of panic in each other's eyes. The thought has come to us late – we're sixty-five minutes into the match, and admittedly we're one-nil up – but we haven't thought it through at all. What happens to Jesse when the Inter-County Schools Under-16s Challenge is over? If he wins, how's he going to feel once the initial burst of elation has faded away? And if he loses (and suddenly, with Thurston playing like a different team, anything could happen), what happens then?

Fortunately, the football is distracting me. At this point, Ryan Dunbar makes one of his better interceptions and wins the ball off their number 6. He passes to Jesse, who's running up centre-field now, and Jesse makes a lovely pass to Callum, just taps it perfectly with the inside of his right foot, and Callum answers with a fantastic little dummy to sneak past the Thurston captain, a black kid called Romeo.

Now, as Luiz explains later, at this point, Callum has two options. He can go for glory – there's one defender between him and the goalie – or he can do the unselfish thing and pass to Shav who has run into a great position, onside but unmarked on the right-hand side of the pitch. So he passes. It's not a bad pass – it's not that high, but it's not a total disaster, and, as he passes, their tall defender with the blond ponytail practically dives through the air like a kamikaze. He heads the ball down, it lands at the feet of Romeo, who turns, raises his eyes momentarily just to check on his target, and lays the ball on for the fleet-footed Fabrizzio.

Freya says you see a lot of animals on the football field. Some run with all the dogged determination of a terrier, others like big cats – panthers – whose spring practically uncoils as they pounce on the ball. But Fabrizzio is like a gazelle. He's athletic and elegant and oh-so-fast. With those slender legs, he can leap through the air and keep moving forward, landing lightly and then making his pass.

'If that kid's not playing for Inter-Milan or Chelsea by the time he's seventeen, I'll take up knitting,' says Andy to Luiz, who nods sagely in agreement.

Fabrizzio streaks away from Mark Chetley who's meant to be marking him ('Nice one, Mark!' someone shouts sarcastically), and, while he's running and just a metre or so outside the box, he kicks the ball at full stretch, and it just takes off. You can practically hear it whoosh past Ali, who can't even get a finger to it. It's like some advert for sportswear off the telly, the ball practically jet-propelled into the back of the net. Cut to shot of the ball bouncing up and down against the netting, mocking Ali and the Joan of Arc defence that Fabrizzio has just shredded. One all.

As you'd expect, their lot go mental. They start bouncing up and down and join in with a chorus of 'la la la la, we're going to win the cup' even though we all know it's a plate. Callum has called the team together for a quick huddle before the game resumes, and he's barking orders at them punctuated with cries of 'C'mon! C'MON!' as he slaps his thigh so hard I can only think 'ouch'. I can hear Rottweiler cupping his hands together too and yelling, 'Strike back, Joan of Arc! Strike back!' It's all getting a bit serious.

'Now we show our boys how we make the noise in Brazil!' shouts Luiz at us all, holding his arms aloft, and then he brings them down defiantly and starts bashing away like crazy on his bongos. Freya joins in with some whooping that I can only describe as a feral child being throttled, and the next thing is, we're all chanting and screaming and singing, 'GIVE US ANOTHER, JOAN OF ARC, GIVE US ANOTHER ONE DO!' The atmosphere is electric.

Both teams are playing at their best now. The boy Fabrizzio is burning up the field with talent and, with a goal under his belt, he's practically alight. He's turning on all the fancy footwork: those flip back passes, cheeky little dummies, and he has amazing ball control. But it's also becoming obvious that, although he's their star player, the rest of the team's not in the same league.

'Granted, they've got some good players,' says Andy, 'but our lot are playing as a team, not as a star vehicle. If they can just keep going, and keep a check on old golden balls, they've got to be in with a shout.'

There's only fifteen minutes or so to go now, and you can see that some of the younger lads are getting weary. Rottweiler has already pulled off our number 8, Jonah, who's not had a good game, and he's replaced him with Paul Paterson who's in Jesse's class at school. I can see Duane Mulholland is warming up on the side too, and I suspect Rottweiller is about to pull Jesse off.

On the left flank, Ryan is starting to make a break through, then flicks the ball across to Raul. Jesse can see a gap in the middle and starts to run into it, as Raul boots the ball towards him. I can see Jesse going up to head it in desperation, giving it his all as usual. Unfortunately, just at the same moment, their dirty number 3 flings his leg forward in what must be the stupidest tackle anyone has ever seen.

The Thurston player's leg connects hard with Jesse's head about a millisecond before the ref gives two long blasts on his whistle, and Jesse hits the ground like a sack of potatoes. If this match were a comic strip, the word *CRUNCH!!!* would be stretched out in colourful capitals as Jesse hits the deck.

Stu and Luiz and I go flying down the terrace to the side of the pitch, but Rottweiler Rubinstein and a woman from St John Ambulance are already with Jesse, doing whatever it is they do with sponges as the ref looks on. The linesman is trying to hold us back, but Stu says, 'That's my kid,' and pushes past him on to the pitch, and Luiz and I follow him on.

'Is he okay?' Stu asks the ref, shoving his way through the huddle that has gathered round Jesse, and the St John Ambulance woman looks up and says, 'Yes, he's back with us. I think he just blacked out there for a minute or two, didn't you, Jesse?'

I'm thinking, Well, that wouldn't be the first time, and

then, Wow, first name terms already. The St John Ambulance woman is calling for a stretcher to get him off the field.

'I'm fine,' Jesse protests, as Luiz and Stu carry him off. 'My head's a bit sore, though.'

'We'll get that checked out at the hospital,' says the St John's woman, who introduces herself as Maggie.

'But I can't leave before the end of the match,' Jesse cries, looking dangerously like he's going to go off on one.

'It's okay if we just hold back for a few minutes, isn't it?' asks Stu. 'It means so much to him – and it is the final.'

'I'm a nurse,' explains Luiz. 'I'll keep an eye on him.'

'Are you his father?' says Maggie looking at Stu.

For a moment Stu looks like he's tempted to ruffle Jesse's hair the way he often does, but considering the nature of his head injury, he keeps his hands in his pockets.

'Something like that,' he says, grabbing Jesse's hand.

By now, dirty number 3 has had his red card and been sent off, presumably to some secure institution for lunatic players, and Duane Mulholland finally gets his chance. Rottweiler has pulled him on to replace Jesse, and it's our free kick. Duane and Callum are both standing behind the ball – we're not quite sure which one is going to take it. The ref blows the whistle, Duane taps the ball, and Callum runs three paces before setting it up beautifully for Mark Chetley, who's come accelerating up the wing and thumps the ball into the back of the net.

Considering Jesse has had another of his near-death experiences, he manages to jump off his stretcher fairly smartly and punches the air in victory. 'Yes!'

I can see Fabbrizio, the Italian stallion, with his head in his hands. They've got it all to do now.

Jesse watches nervously from the side as Maggie wraps a huge bandage round his head. I'm not quite sure what the point of the bandage is, but I'd guess she enjoys bandaging more than football, and to be honest, I don't think Jesse is even remotely aware of what she's up to while he sits and watches the match without blinking. Luiz has passed him an energy drink which he swigs from the side of his mouth in true footballer style, but he keeps jumping up and down whenever Thurston get possession. Fortunately, whoever it is who trains St John Ambulance people seems to teach their staff a whole lot of patience.

It's only another ten minutes with a few more added on for Jesse's black-out, but it's the longest fifteen minutes of my life. When the final whistle is blown, there are more of us up and dancing than you'd see at a school disco. Jesse charges off back to the field with his bandaged head to be greeted by his team-mates like their long-lost lucky mascot – even Duane Mulholland seems to be hugging him and holding him generally responsible for our winning goal, which in a way I suppose he was. There's no way he's going to miss out on the plate presentation.

I can hear Luiz's bongos again (Andy has taken over as principal drummer now) and Jack's whirling his grandad's rattle round his head, while Freya and Mia are screaming 'We Are the Champions' completely off-key at the top of their voices with the rest of the Joan of Arc supporters, who are all on their feet and swaying. The volume is turned to MAX, and everyone's grabbing each other and kissing. They'd be doing a Mexican wave if there were enough supporters in the crowd. I notice that Luiz and Stu are having the kind of embrace you don't normally see on the football field, but no one else seems to notice or care.

The presentation takes place a few minutes later. There seems to be some debate over whether or not their dirty number 3 should get a runners-up medal, having tackled Jesse so vindictively. In the end, the powers that be figure that he's going to get enough stick from his team-mates anyway, so he joins Thurston's line-up and gets his medal, and a big 'BOO!' from our fans, which is no more than he deserves.

When they announce 'Joan of Arc Comprehensive, Inter-County Schools Under-16s Challenge Champions', a huge cheer goes up from the crowd. Freya blasts away on her hooter like some kind of professional noisy person as they line up for the presentation ceremony. They go up one by one to receive their medals from the Lady Mayor, who's obviously styled herself on the Queen, even down to the concrete perm, handbag and white gloves. She has a smile and a nod and a word with each of the team, in a suitably regal manner. She looks concerned when it's Jesse's turn to take his medal – she must be asking about his head because he points to the bandage and does his brave little soldier face – then he takes the medal, turns to wave at us lot, and we all scream a bit more.

'Atta boy!' shouts Polly, and Jack and Freya are at their rattle and hooter again in some kind of insane effort to try and break the sound barrier. When Callum finally lifts the plate, all hell breaks loose. There are cameras flashing, loo rolls flying, the crowd is cheering – even the Thurston lot seem genuinely pleased – and the Joan of Arc boys hoist Jesse up on their shoulders and parade him around for a bit as he holds the silver trophy above his head and kisses it and poses for the crowd.

And I think, he won the plate, Mum. He bloody won it.

After the endless laps of honour, our lot finally head off to the changing rooms, led by Rottweiler Rubinstein who looks like he has ruptured a few facial muscles with all the smiling he's done this afternoon.

Half an hour later, Jesse eventually emerges, looking like Tutankhamen's concussed younger brother. The bandage is a bit damper now and someone has scrawled *CHAMPS* across the top in felt-tip pen, but it's still wrapped round his head. Sort of.

'I was thinking maybe all down to Papa Giorgio's for a celebratory pizza?' suggests Stu.

'Do you think they'll let us in?' says Polly. 'We look like extras from Michael Jackson's 'Thriller' video.'

She's right. We're all up for it, carrying on the party atmosphere, but we look a right state. Freya's hat is a bit ropey round the edges now, but she's still refusing to take it off, and the rest of us have blood, sweat and tears (well okay, not blood, but red hair paint) smeared round our faces.

'They'll let us in,' says Luiz optimistically. 'We have our lucky mascot, don't we?'

'Isn't he meant to be going to the hospital?' I ask Stu. 'That Maggie – the St John Ambulance woman – said he needs getting the once-over from a doctor.'

'I'll take him down later when I start my shift,' says Luiz. 'We gonna get you checked out, eh, Ronaldo?'

'Stop fussing,' moans Jesse, examining his medal. 'I'm fine.'

'Hey, Jesse,' I call over to him as we walk towards the car park. 'There's somebody we ought to phone to tell the good news, you know?'

His face drops. He looks dead worried, and starts fiddling with his bandage.

'Not Mrs McLafferty . . .'

'No, not Mrs McLafferty, you dweeb,' I tell him. 'Dad. I bet he'd like to know. We should call Dad.'

Stu chucks me his mobile.

'Good idea, guys,' he smiles. 'He's in there under "I" for Ian.'

'Okay,' says Jesse, 'but I want to talk to him first.'